It looked like a black puddle. Solomon tried to step backwards, but Cowl Monkshood was behind him and pushed Solomon a little more forward.

As Solomon was forced to move forward, the black slimy thing jumped up in to the air. For a few moments it seemed to hover over Solomon's head. Solomon looked up at it and before he could make a sound, the black thing dropped onto his face smothering him, covering his face completely.

After a minute it had covered him from head to toe. Solomon looked like a black statue covered in oil. Unlike oil, this thing was alive.

If I had children of my own this would have been a great story to read to them before bed. It started off a bit slow, as most 1st-in-a-series books do when the author is 'world-building', but hang in there, as the story starts to move right along the further you get into it and I found it hard to put down.

The author was able to create a very descriptive 'other world' in the woods and was able to transport me there with his writing. I also enjoyed the very creative names he came up with for the fairies and mythical creatures.

Alison Pensy.
Author of the Custodian Novels
The Amulet, The Emerald Staff and The Cypher Wheel

I recently completed The Faeries of Birchover Wood . It is an exquisite children's book but it is not only for children. It is extremely imaginative and creative. The faeries are unique. He has created personalities and the descriptions and names of each one that are beautiful. You won't want it to end.

Shana Dines.
Author of American Ghost Stories.

This is an incredible fantasy/adventure story. I was swept up into the adventure early in the story by the strong plot line and the strong characters of this other world.

The author has created a magnificent world of faeries, dragons, oakmen, and other great fantasy characters that dwell along side humans. If you have never believed that magical creatures live in the forests, you will now.

Diane Mae Robinson.
Winner of the Lieutenant Governor of Alberta Emerging Artist
Award Literary Arts 2012 and author of Sir Princess Petra

*Ian Rutter's writing strikes a chord with both children and adults
in The Faeries of Birchover Wood, Book 1. The Bad is very very
Bad, and in the first part of the book, we learn how bad it is. The
Faeries of Birchover Wood is a book for everyone.*

L. Lee Scott
Author of Storm Bourne

The Faeries of Birchover Wood

The Bad

Book One

by

Ian S. Rutter

Table of Contents

Poem – The Magic Never Ends

Dedication

Dedicated to my son, Solomon.
Who even before his birth
inspired me to write this story.

To my wife, Mini.
She always thought I could and should.

Thanks Dad for the happy, smiley poem.
I would never of thought up something like that.

This story is also for my great friend Winnie.

Fond memories

Poem

*A*s I sat amongst the trees one day, my eyes were

drawn to things that swayed amongst the boughs and leaves. I saw flitting from tree to tree, little bodies with wings that moved so fast the human eyes could not catch.

As I looked a ball of mist appeared as if a meeting had occurred. And in a flash it flew away to hide behind the boughs and leaves that kept all of them safe.

I stared, three little beings came floating down to search me out upon the ground. I felt no fear just a calmness all around, and then a canopy of light covered the ground.

Visions I had and visions I could see, mythical creatures appeared to me. Abby Lubbers and the Apple Tree Man. Barguest, Black Annis and Boggarts were the start. Bogies, Brownies and the Bucca Bucca Boo came next, followed by Derricks and Dobbies with Feriers, Gable Rathchets, Galley-Begger and Gally Trot.

I looked and smiled as well as sweat, for fear and excitement were taking me. A journey that was not yet at an end.

Hairy Jacks, Hinkey Punk, with Knockers and Knuckers all were so clear. Necken and Nixies, Oakmen and Old Bloody Bones, my mind was amazed by the spirits that were here.

More came and showed themselves to me. I was aghast by the sight and so I continued to peer. Padfoot, Peg O'Nell, the Peg Powler, Pinkets and Piskies and Pixies flying around. With Portune standing only an inch high, everything was a wonder. Then they all looked at me.

Shag Foal and Spriggans came over to see. Next there was Thrummy Cap and the Tiddy Ones. Waffs and Wight and my favourite Will o the Wisp. I was happy to be among the creatures of the night.

It was time to say goodbye and my dream was coming to an end. All that stood around me promised that I would never forget.

Now that you have been touched by the magic of the creatures, forever you will see them and never forget.

I closed my eyes and counted to three. I opened them and was back in my room. A book called Mythical Creatures was next to me.

From that time on and to this present day, I still visit my friends in the woods of Birchover.

The magic never ends.

1

- HUNGRY -

The sky was covered in a carpet of brilliant blue, stretching as far as the eye could see. Not even a cloud to break the perfect covering. All was peaceful in the sky, but on the ground it was a different story.

The land was covered in lush sweet green grass and soft to the touch. Each blade of grass gently swayed as the invisible stroking hand of a breeze tickled it.

Cows were grazing, chewing the grass like it was the best thing they've ever eaten. The sound of ripping and the crunching of grass between teeth was being carried by the wind. All the cows were content with their free meal unaware that something was lurking close by.

This something, this thing was unlike any beast that had walked, crawled or slithered. It had no real defining physical form. It was black as the night and looked like what could be described as very thick mud.

It moved like a caterpillar, changing shape from flat to bulbous so that it could travel from one place to another. If you saw it you would be forgiven for saying that it resembled a giant slug. It belched, bulged, slithered and slimed.

Constantly hungry, it kept looking for food so that it could grow and gain strength. The beast wasn't dumb, nor was it without purpose. It had a plan and it needed to eat more, a lot more before it was strong enough to meet its final victims and fulfil an obsession. The obsession for power to rule over everyone.

This hulk of badness was simply that, bad. There was nothing good about it. Goodness could never come from it. It was soulless. Maybe it was a representation of all that was bad in the world, or it was a virus that had mutated into something larger, more dangerous. Whatever it was or wherever it came from, the Bad, the name that it can be described as, had only one purpose, to eat anything living and then grow.

Slithering its way across the grassy land of a farmer's field, the Bad slowly crept closer and closer towards a cow that was peacefully grazing on the lush green grass. It stopped slithering, sensing the cow was feeling a little weary. The munching cow raised its head to see if anything was approaching. Seeing nothing strange, the cow lowered its head back down to drown in mouthfuls of sweet juicy grass. Once the cow settled back munching away at the free feast, the Bad continued its journey towards its prey.

Only a few feet away from the cow, the Bad slowly sucked in air, expanding its black sticky mass giving itself enough energy to lunge at its chosen prey.

The cow stopped munching. The grass stopped swaying and without warning, a loud shrieking noise from behind the cow erupted. It was a sound like a skidding car on a dry road. The cow threw its head up to try and see what was making the noise, at the same time jumping forward to try and outrun the invisible sound. The cow couldn't move fast enough, and in the corner of its big round eyes it saw what made the noise.

A black muddy form jumped into the air, some of its body still clinging to the ground as to keep balance.

Within a few seconds, the horrible dirty form touched the cow. As its mass of slime started to take a grip of the defenceless animal, the rest of its body left the ground. Like a spring desperate to get back into shape, the rest of the formless beast fell upon the cow. In the blink of an eye the cow was covered in what looked like black slime.

The eyes of the cow opened as wide as they could just from sheer fright. Its cries drowned out by the smothering, sticky substance that shaped itself around the cow, until all that was left was a silhouette of its shape. Black as the night sky it was clearly visible with the sun shinning brightly.

The Bad rippled as if it was swallowing. The rippling effect started at one end, peaked in the middle and then died down at the other end. As this movement continued, a loud sound could be heard and the shape of the cow disappeared with each passing rippling effect.

A few minutes later as the body of the cow had been consumed, the black mass slowly sank to the ground until it just looked like a mound of mud. Motionless, glistening in the sun.

A few moments passed and the mound of living mud seemed to shiver, as if it had been hit by a cold wind. The shivering stopped, then the Bad moved across the grassy field towards another cow.

It never felt content or full, pity or remorse. It didn't care what it ate. It knew that the more it ate the faster and bigger it grew. And it wanted to be so very big, before the time came to show itself and what it was capable of.

2

-SIGHTINGS -

T he age of magic and mysticism was believable at one time. Humans and faeries were friends and England was in a time when folklore, myths and legends were born from great acts of chivalry. Knights were abundant, and the King was respected by both his subordinates and the animals of the land.

At that time, certain myths were true such as faeries and they had been around longer than anyone could remember. Humans and myths lived together side by side in harmony. As both groups lived off the land both helped each other.

The faeries protected the domestic animals and the harvest, and humans were very careful as to what was cut down from the woodlands. For England, it was a very prosperous and peaceful period in time until something started to stir.

People could be heard saying strange things about cattle disappearing. Fields of hay having strange blackish muddy trails. Horses refused to go in a certain direction running scared from something that couldn't be seen. All this was accepted as country folk, reading into something that really was just a bunch of nonsense and superstition. As time went on so the stories seemed to disappear.

Everyone and everything got on with whatever was needed to be done. But, within the community of faeries some of the elders were feeling slightly worried. Therefore, they sent out scouts to look for what was behind the stories. Sadly, all the scouts reported nothing but the odd bone or black trail of mud. Nothing else could be found. The scouts were called off but the word was to keep all senses alert, in-case anything unusual should happen.

One particular elder of great age and wisdom, knew that what they were seeking would one day show itself. It wasn't long before the Bad did show itself.

It started by ravaging small villages. Many people tried to attack it with simple weapons such as, pitch forks, sheers and home made spears but it did no good. The black veil of mud like substance would drown the attackers by covering them in its black sticky body.

When the Bad moved on, all that remained were corpses, thin as a stick, white as chalk and with an expression of sheer fright frozen to their faces.

One time, a village had lookouts on the watch readying themselves for the thing to come. The spotters as they were known, had been looking for days until one shouted, "IT'S HERE!"

The Bad was spotted and the whole village prepared itself. They had the usual farming tools at hand as well as five catapults they had made. The ends of these catapults were filled with hay soaked in black oil ready to be lit.

The village had about 200 men and women as well as children. Anyone strong enough to pick up a weapon stood facing the direction the Bad was coming from.

The head of the village looked around and noticed there was no sound in the air. Not even a cluster of black ravens or crows were flying. It was to be a black day.

He said to himself, "Death is coming. May God have mercy on us all."

Just over the far hill in the distance, everyone saw a dark

mass of a thing moving forward. It was huge! Black and solid, leaving a trail of black slime behind as it moved forward towards the village.

"READY!" the village head shouted.

Everyone stiffened their stance. The five catapults were loaded with bales of hay dripping in black oil. The men in charge of lighting them were shaking with fear. There were a dozen men with bows and flaming arrows at the ready. The whole village was standing in a long curved line, ready to hit the oncoming nothingness from every angle.

The men, women and children who had volunteered to stand and fight stood looking at the thing that was coming forward, faster and faster towards them.

In front of the villages was a stone wall they had built a few days before. Hope rested on the wall that it would stop it, or at least slow the beast down.

"CATAPULTS. READY!"

The village head screamed the order, and the five catapults with bales of hay loaded were lit. Immediately, the bales of hay roared with intensity, and the men in charge of operating them had to step back so as not to be scorched by the red hot flames. The village head had his hand raised high. Those at the catapults were waiting for the order. Seconds seemed like hours, everyone sweating with fear.

All the animals had gone taken from the village. All that remained was silence, just the occasional crackling sound from the dry burning hay. Not even a cool breeze could be felt. Death was coming and it was coming fast.

"FIRE!"

The village head shouted the order at the same time bringing his arm down with great speed.

The men at the catapults pulled the levers hard. With a thundering noise the bales of hay left the catapults and ripped across the bright blue sky, leaving a black thick line of smoke. Within seconds there were five fire balls screaming through the air, heading for the shapeless thing ready to devour the Bad with fire.

BOOM! Three bails of hay hit the ground with a sound that

could be heard for miles. Fire spread across the field in front of the speeding beast. The fire rose high into the air blocking the path of the oncoming evil. The other two fiery bales of hay hit the Bad fast and hard. Some of the villagers cheered but the fire balls blew apart as they hit the oncoming monster, spreading fire in all directions, burning on top of the beast and then dying out quickly.

"FIRE. AGAIN!"

Another five missiles of burning hay were flying high into the sky. This time all five hit the shapeless beast.

Five scorching hot fire balls slammed hard into the beast. At the same time, the charging beast hit the wall of fire that was created a few moments before. With the wall of fire and the fire balls engulfing the Bad, it became one gigantic ball of black and orange fire. It let out a deep growling scream, not of pain but of anger. This scream of anger quickly turned into a burst of speed. The Bad rapidly shot forward leaving a trail of fire. It was now heading straight for the village.

The village head shouted a command and the line of people started to slowly back away. But then, some of villagers feeling fearful started to run away from the beast and into the village. Some of the men stood their ground, until they saw the shapeless black mass smash through the wall like it was made of grass. Boulders flew through the air crashing to the ground. A few of the rocks came crashing on some men who tried to run out of the way.

The men who were operating the catapults were the first to be hit by the Bad. It showed no mercy.

Rising high into the air, its form blocked out the sun from the men who were looking up at it. Without time to spare, the men tried to run and before they made two feet, it came crashing down upon them. All that was heard was a loud scream then a dull thud. People screamed all around. Some ran back into their homes and some brave souls stood to fight the formless beast.

They stood on the spot throwing spears, pitchforks, rakes and rocks at the thing. Only to see that everything that they threw was just sucked into its hulking black mass. Without hesitation, long black tentacles shot out from the Bad in all directions. At amazing speed the tentacles caught hold of people and dragged

16

them into its body. As every victim was caught and pulled into the black slimy body, so its size increased.

The beast was still smoking from the fire and behind it was the trail it left behind, which was still alight.

Some people in sheer desperation to get away ran into the fire and were gobbled up by the flames.

Tentacles of varying lengths and thickness were still shooting out of the beast, grabbing people then throwing them up into the air. As if time slowed down the falling victims fell into the hulking mass of a body. Some of the tentacles flattened out and were used to swipe away homes to reveal the occupants, who were found shuddering in a corner, defenceless. A few seconds later the building was destroyed and the occupants were taken.

The destruction of the village and the mass taking of the villagers was over in less than twenty minutes. The village was left in a pile of rubble with a few fires burning away. The physical sign of the beast, was a long line of black slime and burnt soil left in its wake of carnage. As before, when it had finished it disappeared without a trace.

Silence returned to the village as did a breeze. Ravens were picking on what was left, but something stirred in the background causing the ravens to fly away. A movement indicating the Bad was returning?

It wasn't the Bad. It was a young child of about fourteen years old, who had survived by diving for cover under a pile of fallen rocks. There he stayed silent, not moving an inch. A witness to the destruction of his home and people. The boy was forced to watch until the Bad had gone. There was nothing he could do.

A mist of dense black smoke blew across the land making it difficult to see.

The boy got up dazed and confused wondering if there were any other survivors.

Scared and shaking with fear, he fell to the ground and started to cry until his eyes became dry and his lungs started to hurt. With nothing else to do and with what seemed like all hope lost, the young boy picked himself up and started his long lonely walk to try and find help.

After a few hours of wandering, the boy was picked up by a group of the King's guards. They listened to the boy's story and after giving him food and water, they immediately took him back to the capital at full gallop.

It took a few days to get back to the King and once they did, the boy was taken care off.

After being told of the plight of the boy's village, as well as all the other stories of this mysterious beast roaming the land, a plan of action was organised.

It was time for battle.

3

- THE MEETING -

Something had to be done, and it was apparent the normal tactics for battle would be useless, especially when one of the King's knights came back looking like a skeleton still attached to his horse. That was a sign that the Bad was indeed powerful, for if it could defeat a knight blessed by God, then the King needed God like powers to defeat the Bad.

The King knew about the mythical beasts that dwelt upon the land. He knew that the beast that was causing havoc was no ordinary beast, and to face it the King would need special knowledge on how to defeat it. He called upon the enchanted beasts of the land and all answered his cry for help.

Faeries or fae as some would have them known. Boggarts, shape shifting goblins called Brags. Derricks the size of dwarfs. Knockers, mine spirits from Cornwall. Swamp dragons called Knuckers and many others that had to be seen to be believed. The King was moved and humbled by what had gathered outside his court yard.

On the day when all the myths came forth a pact was made. A pact that was to last until time itself would end. This pact would ensure that as long as mankind continued to live with nature, man, myth, folklore and legend would be remembered. Everything would live with each other having respect and admiration for the other.

For the faeries, the one who represented them was called Elder Perennial Swallowtail. He had a mind unlike any other faery that had come before him. His knowledge of magic was vast, having even taught some humans the wonderful qualities of plants and herbs that grew around the countryside.

He had an idea of what the Bad was and even had an idea of how to defeat it. He sort council with the King and the King accepted.

Elder Perennial Swallowtail introduced himself to the King. To make communication a little easier, Elder Swallowtail whispered a few words to himself, and almost immediately the faery was nearly the same height as the king. All the King saw was a slight blurry image and the faery changed from being just a size of an apple, to the size of an adult. They both spoke for hours until day turned into night and night turned into day.

They both came out of a sealed room guarded by twelve knights dressed in pure white armour. Each guard stood still with a sword held in their right hand. A shield held in their left. It had a picture of a lion's head and the words, 'In Deus Nos Reperio, Vires Quod Rex Rgis Nos, Reperio Veneratio' (*In God we find strength and our King we find honour*) written around its frame.

The King and Elder Swallowtail stood to greet all the beasts and men who served under the King. Everyone stood up and looked at the King, and as they did they could all see an aura of light shining brightly around him.

The King spoke to everyone in the great room of his castle. As he spoke his voice echoed throughout the room.

"Elder Perennial Swallowtail and I, have spoken about a great many things."

The King's voice seemed concerned but still had an authority to it.

"We believe the only way to fight this cursed evil is to pull together our beliefs, and combine them into one very powerful spell of goodness. A pure spell that will be too powerful for this evil beast to fight against."

There came a lot of mumbling from everyone in the room. To quieten the noise, Elder Swallowtail's glow increased and a little humming sound could be heard. This not only made everyone quiet but seemed to give the King added strength.

It was decided that a member from each of the animals, or mythical creatures would be selected to contribute to the spell.

From the faeries there came ancient herbs. From the swamp dragons came a golden claw, known as the Claw of Compassion. Legend has it that anyone who has the claw will be able to ride the backs of any dragon, even the most vicious. From the boggarts, came a vase of essence that is said to help anyone shape shift. Next, a goblin gave a leather chest covering that was worn by the great goblin king, King Grak Ig Ven. The derricks gave the sweetest meats from Cornwall. The King himself gave writings on the finest silk paper. Stories of great chivalry, honesty and bravery. Also, he gave a sword to the spell a symbol of righteousness.

All the items were wrapped up inside a satchel made from spiders' silk, woven by the hands of five hundred female faeries. Then a glass containing one breath of dragon's fire was to be thrown onto the package of items to seal them and consummate the spell.

As the glass of dragon's fire was thrown, it hit the satchel shattering the glass spreading the fire, devouring the satchel. A green and blue flame erupted filling the empty space of the room. Then it formed a long spiral of fire.

The satchel, engulfed by the fire rose into the air hovering in the centre of the room. The spiral of fire was now a ball of green and blue flames, with the satchel in the middle of this amazing spectacle.

Elder Swallowtail moved forward saying a few words quietly. He tossed some water that he carried in a container at the flames. As the water hit the flames, a brilliant flash of green, blue and red light erupted. The flames and satchel fell to the ground and

21

what was left was a crystal ball. Inside it everyone could see a rainbow of colours whirling around like a mist.

Elder Swallowtail picked up the ball, which was now the size of a human hand and gave it to the King.

"Righteous King of this country," he said, "this is for you and you alone to use."

The King took the ball, which had no weight but felt as solid as steel.

"I will use it for the good of this country, and for every living thing that walks up on the soil, flies in the sky or swims in the sea." he replied.

Everyone looked at the King and with raised fists saluted and cheered him.

Moments later and with the crystal ball in his hand, the King faced his huge army that had formed outside the castle. Wearing his battle armour and sitting on his white and black Clydesdale, he turned his attention to the army that represented every living creature that lived in England.

"My friends," he paused in thought, "do not look up on me as a saviour. Today we will save one another. We will fight an evil that threatens the very existence of what we hold dear. We will overcome that beast and send it back to where it came from. And never will we see it again."

The King looked round to all that was in front of him.

"We will not give in. We will not be afraid of fear. We will be fear itself to that, that comes forth and tries to take away what we love."

The adrenaline in everyone was flowing.

"An evil such as that, which we have never seen before can not be permitted to live. I, like you will put my life down if it means all other life may live. May God be on our side, and may we succeed so that we can celebrate with HONOUR!"

The King's horse reared its front legs high into the air, and an army of numbers that were too many to count cheered out loud, shaking the very foundations of the King's home.

The King's army was ready.

The King's knights, foot soldiers and archers were all

standing to attention. The beasts of myths were fearless and ready for war.

A large group of gold and bronze coloured dragons flew overhead. Some had landed standing at the back of the army with their wings outstretched, as if they were warming them from the heat of the sun. Goblins readied themselves sharpening their battle axes.

Faeries flew around everyone handing out small sacks to be worn around the neck. Inside these sacks, the herb Absinthe. An ancient herb that has always been used to protect the wearer from evil.

Blurrs and afancs gathered together. Majestic griffins had arrived and allowed some soldiers to be riders.

The huge army separated into two halves. The King on his horse rode through the centre inspecting his army. As he was inspecting his fearless men his mind started to think.

He was the King of the greatest nation that had ever lived. He and his men had over come hordes of barbarians from other countries. He, as well as his forefathers had marched against armies of greater size, knowing that this land was blessed by God. Since the one who has been anointed King or Queen of England and sits on a throne upon the Bethel Stone, because of that, England can and will never be ruled by a foreign invader.

In the King's mind, this new invader had no such ideas about rule. It seemed to have come from nowhere and its intentions were on destroying everything. It had to be stopped at any cost.

The King was now at the front of the army. His men were giving their service to him at no cost. He looked at them and gave the order.

"MARCH!"

With perfect timing, everything that held a weapon slammed its right foot down hard to the ground, creating an eruption of sound. The army moved forward walking through the castle's gates towards the last known destination of the Bad.

4

- THE BATTLE -

F or a few days the vast army of men and myths walked on. Everyone and everything had one thing on their mind, the survival of its kind against an enemy that had proved to be very elusive. Every so often, scouts would be sent out and ordered to report back on any unusual activities or sightings.

Four groups of men were selected. Each group having four men. Each of the groups were sent in a Northern, Southern, Western and Eastern direction. They had the fastest horses and to not slow the horses down, they rode with very little protection, only carrying a sword and the emblem of the King on the chest plate of their uniform. Each group also had a Peregrine Falcon flying with them. Every rider knew what to do if he spotted the beast.

The group was to make a positive sighting, then tag the falcon with a message stipulating the exact location of the beast at that time. Then two men would trail the beast, while the other two of the group would gallop as fast as they could back to the King, making sure the message was delivered. Once they had met up with the King's army, they would direct the army to the last known location of the beast.

The groups were sent out and the King waited patiently for word of the enemy. It was an unsettling time and to pass the time, the King frequently talked to Elder Perennial Swallowtail about life as a faery and the lifestyle they lived. The King was most interested and was known as one who was keen on new ideas and cultures. Just then a voice in the background broke his conversation with Elder Swallowtail.

"LOOK! THE FALCON. IT'S HERE!"

Everyone looked at the man who was shouting. He was pointing at the sky.

The falcon came swooping down. Not a sound could be heard. Only a perfectly formed body could be seen. A man who had been trained with the falcon raised his head and whistled. Immediately, the falcon turned direction and headed for the whistling man. The falcon swooped low to the ground only inches from touching it. Within a few feet of the man's raised arm, the falcon shot up lifting its talons and gently landing on the man's arm that was covered in a thick leather glove.

After giving the falcon some well earned fresh meat, the man unclipped the message that was tied to the falcons leg. He immediately gave the message to the King who was now standing next to him.

The King unwrapped the message and read it.

*Northern Group. Have spotted the beast
near the village of Birchover.*

Two men are on the way to meet you

My comrade and I, will follow the beast

Will try and slow it down until you arrive

After the King read it everyone knew what to do.

"Everyone, ready yourselves for Birchover. We ride in five minutes."

The Kings voice echoed through the whole camp of men, and not one wasted any time. War was at hand.

The army marched hard. On the way, the army met the two scouts coming back to report on the sighting. The two scouts led the way and after a few days, they were very close to Birchover village.

On the way to Birchover the scouts described what they had seen. A huge mass of black and brown mud like substance. They had witnessed a few people who had tried to fight it but were grabbed and sucked into its body. The King listened intently and reassured his men that nothing was unstoppable.

The army had now positioned itself within a wood just outside the village. From this position the King could see what was happening. His view was clear. No Bad. No black mass. Nothing.

He ordered the falcon to be let loose, in case his scouts were hiding and wanted to know if they had arrived. The bird soared into the air scouring the sky. It saw something and swooped down, but before it could change direction it was grabbed from the sky and devoured. That was the sign the Bad was here.

The King sent messages telling his men to take position and

wait on his command. They were ready to move. As soon as his men gave a signal that they were all ready, the King raised his sword and the whole group moved forward in perfect timing.

The plan was to surround the beast and attack it from all sides, to see if a weakness could be found. The whole troop of men and myth moved forward, all weapons at the ready. The ground rumbled under the constant pounding of the army's feet. The noise of their presence filtered back to the Bad. It had now turned direction and headed for the King and his men.

The King saw the Bad in full view for the first time.

"What in heaven is it?" he asked himself.

The army split into four different sections. Each section had an equal number of men and mythical creatures. The faeries, flying swamp dragons and those that could fly took to the sky. The plan, to attack fast, viciously and without mercy.

The first thing to hit the Bad was a sky full of arrows. They poured down like hailstones only much deadlier and more accurate. For the first assortment of arrows, there were no less than a thousand screeching through the air in one go. The sky became black and the accuracy was unquestionable. All the arrows hit their intended target. As every arrow penetrated the mass of slime, everyone from the army looked. For a few seconds the Bad paused as the arrows stuck out protruding from the body, making the slimy beast look like an over grown hedgehog. Then a sound like a long breath sucked in air and the arrows started to sink in and disappear.

A second assortment of arrows were at the ready.

"FIRE!" the King commanded.

The arrows were set free. This time even more were streaming through the air, and before they had hit their target, a third lot of arrows were following in the air. The heads of these arrows were on fire. Like a stealth missile every single arrow hit the black and brown mass. The arrows with burning heads hit the black beast and the fire hissed. Again, all the arrows were sucked in.

The King shouted an order and all horses galloped at full speed, with the King at the forefront of the stampede. Running soldiers with swords drawn were screaming at the top of their voices. Goblins and other mythical creatures charged forward screaming in their own tongue. The land was a noise of fear and heroism.

Three groups ran ahead and split up. One group split to the left side. One group split to the right, and the third group galloped ahead. They were to surround the Bad. The King and his group would hit what they presumed was the front. As the King and his men rushed forward, five dragons glided effortlessly above and ahead of them.

The King shouted, "TAKE THAT THING DOWN!"

With one flap of their giant wings the dragons sped forward. Two broke away. One to the left and one to the right. The remaining three formed a triangle formation. The three let out a soul destroying burst of fire at the Bad covering it completely. The heat was so hot, that it would have fried a man within a second of coming into contact with it. The other two dragons after seeing their comrades fly off, swooped in with outstretched talons bigger than a house. Plunging their claws deep into the black and brown burning mass, they pulled large chunks of the stuff out as they flew past.

The Bad didn't move didn't even make a sound, it just shuddered.

The dragons threw away what they had ripped out from the Bad, and as soon as the stuff hit the ground it quickly moved in the direction where the Bad was and rejoined it. The five dragons roared in the sky having their prize deceive them. They turned around and came for another pass. This time the Bad was ready.

As two dragons breathed and spat their fire the Bad shot out of the way. The dragons missed their intended target and instead, they hit a few buildings blowing them up and sending rocks shooting into the sky. The other three dragons quickly veered away, but as they passed the Bad it shot out a huge tentacle, which grabbed the tail of one of the passing dragons. The dragon that got caught jerked viciously in the air. It roared and with its wings flapping at an increased rate, it was finding it more and more difficult to stay in the air.

A thousand arrows were set free and hit the Bad but it did

nothing.

The four remaining dragons came around and at an increased speed, headed for the tentacle.

The two leading dragons blew out fire balls, which were the size of horse drawn carriages. Four, five, six fire balls flew fast and hard at the tentacle hitting it with pinpoint accuracy. The fire balls blasted apart when they hit the tentacle, and the fire spread up and down the long black grip.

As the tentacle burned with such intense heat it started to drip like hot wax, instantly starting small fires as they hit the ground.

The other two dragons charged forward, and with two massive flaps of their wings increased their speed and smashed themselves into the burning melting tentacle. The dragons hit the tentacle hard blasting it apart by their sheer speed. This immediately set the captured dragon free. As the five dragons flew higher into the sky the Bad made a noise, which was the start of its size increasing ten fold.

The dragons had come around and were warier of this new adversary.

The King's army had now surrounded the beast, and were shooting it with arrows and hand made balls of burning hay, held in slings. At once, about fifty were thrown at the beast then as the riders shot past the black mass, another fifty rode on and swung their weapons. This happened with another two assortment of riders. About two hundred balls of burning hay hit the beast, sizzling upon impact then disappearing into the bulging body. It was then the beast started to attack the army.

Everyone heard the noise but no-one expected what came.

The Bad seemed to make a noise similar to air being sucked in very fast. The noise ceased, a pause and all of a sudden hundreds of black oily balls the size of a man's head shot out of the beast at incredible speed. The black round mass of projectiles hit their intended victims knocking them off their horses.

The riders hit the ground hard, trying to wipe the black stuff off their bodies as they tried to stand up. The black balls that hit them had other intentions rather than just knocking them off their horses. The black mass clung to the men like glue, and like a long springy rope the black ball stretched itself, and started to drag its victim towards the huge black mass that it had come from. The men were being dragged one by one into the body of the Bad.

"My God!" the King exclaimed, seeing some of his men being pulled to their death.

"DO SOMETHING! HELP THEM" he cried out.

Some of the riders got off their horses to try and help their fallen comrades. Another barrage of black balls hit them and started to drag them to the body also. The King picked up a flaming arrow, loaded it onto a bow, pulled the bow string and let the arrow fly. The arrow was aimed right at one of the black balls that had attached itself to one of his men. The arrow with its sharp metallic head on fire spun in the air and with pin point accuracy, hit the black ball, which had stretched itself quite thinly on the ground. The arrow buried itself into the slime, but instead of being sucked in, the stretched black ball suddenly screeched letting go of the man it was dragging.

The King witnessed that the black thing did not die. It quickly scurried back to its master, rejoining the big bulky black beast that had spit it out.

"BURNING ARROWS! Aim for the black stuff on the men," the King ordered. "QUICKLY!"

Without hesitation, hundreds of arrows screeched through the air and into the black blobs. As with the first one, every black blob screeched letting go of its victim and scurried back to its master.

The Bad sensed it had been thwarted of its prey and raised itself high into the air. Without entirely leaving the ground, the Bad stretched most of its body travelling a huge distance in seconds. It came crashing down, landing upon unsuspecting riders and their horses. Without a blink of an eye, the Bad shot out a hundred tentacles of varying length and thickness in all directions. It was like a black star exploding. After a few seconds each tentacle had grabbed a man.

The King and all other beasts saw a hundred men plucked from their horses, as well as the horses themselves, being lifted off the ground and dragged into the ever expanding mass of black slime.

The King looked at Elder Perennial Swallowtail who was by his side.

With eyes of desperation he said, "I have to do something."

Elder Perennial Swallowtail looked at the King and said to him, "King, you carry the answer with you."

The King immediately grabbed the package that had been made in the castle and as before, it was as light as a feather but felt solid. This time it was different. The ball was changing shape in the King's hand. For a second this confused the King until he saw something fly past him.

The Bad had shot a tentacle out to grab the King and upon seeing this, seven quick reacting soldiers had pulled out their bow and arrows. With the heads of the arrows now on fire, the archers released the arrows at the same time. All the arrows hit the tentacle just as it was about to grab the King. The burning heads of the arrows burned the tentacle and it shot back. The seven riders rode side by side the King and understood his plan.

All around the King, men, myths and legends fought. Dragons blew fire balls onto the beast. Trolls fought hacking away with ancient battle axes, and faeries conjured multicoloured beams of light that they shot at the Bad. The parts of the monstrous beast that were hit by the light turned to stone. Sadly, the effect only lasted seconds. Everyone saw that the Bad was able to regenerate the damaged area. Once it did, it continued to attack like nothing had happened.

The King grabbed an arrow and the magical ball. As soon as the ball came into contact with the arrow, it was as if the ball knew what to do. It stretched itself to the full length of the arrow. Then it submerged the weapon within itself, turning itself into an arrow of mystical light. The King held a new weapon that would fly longer, further and deeper into the belly of the Bad. As he looked at it he knew what he had to do.

High in the sky the dragons were still raging war on the Bad. Helping the army they would spit dragon fire on the tentacles that shot out. It quickly got around that fire could slow the

31

tentacles down, so the dragons did all they could to help out.

The King sent word that he wanted to ride the back of one of the golden dragons, and quickly the largest of the dragons swooped down, motioning to the King to ride towards the trees that were in the background. Hastily, the king and the dragon got to the trees and after landing, the dragon listened to what he was told understanding the plan of action.

"In this war, I am your servant," the huge golden dragon called Gerth said to the King.

"Sit on my neck and let us end this war."

Elder Perennial Swallowtail flew over and quickly chanted a spell.

"Brancha Oak Greesarda"

Branches from the surrounding trees slithered to the feet of the King and quickly formed a makeshift saddle. It was tied around the neck of Gerth and the King was ready to ride.

The King had a feeling of reassurance when he sat on the neck of the dragon. Secure and protected. Maybe it was because the dragon was big, bold and beautiful. Or maybe it was that they would be flying high in the sky. Whatever it was, the King had a weapon to end this war and to see things were put right.

With one flap of his enormous wings the dragon lifted off into the air, and the two were quickly gaining speed and height. For a brief moment, the King felt he was free and understood what it was like to be a bird.

From high up he looked at the state of the battle. His brave men fighting to preserve life as they knew it to be, and the other creatures were fighting with a tenacity that made him proud that there was peace among all living creatures, and they were on his side.

"Get ready, King," Gerth said, who was now joined by the other four golden dragons.

The King looked and on each of his sides there were two dragons. The five dragons filled the sky with an awesome array of flying. It was magnificent to see.

The King readied his bow and arrow, which sparkled and shone colours of blues, reds, purples, greens and yellows in the sunlight. The feeling in his hands was of power for the greater good.

He steadied his hands and clasped the arrow on the bow, pulling the bow string as tight as possible. The creaking sound of the bow strings and the tension in his arms were enough for him to yell, "I'M READY!"

The dragon smiled and all five dived towards the black mass that was waiting for the them. The four dragons at the side moved ahead slightly, and with a head movement from Gerth, the dragon the King was sitting on, the four dragons blasted the black beast with fire that was so intense, the men on the ground had to jump for cover or they would have been cooked to a cinder.

The fire breath hit the Bad and this time everyone heard a scream coming from inside it.

The whole mass of a monster was covered in flames. The Bad tried to move and as it did, the fire of the dragons moved with it.

Gerth shouted to the king, "When my fellow dragons move away, then it's your turn to shoot the arrow."

The King shouted back, "JUST GIVE ME A CLEAR SHOT!"

The dragon smiled liking his companion's fighting spirit.

The four dragons that had flown ahead closed their mouths and instantly changed direction, just missing the ground as they scooped up and headed back to the sky. Gerth lowered his head a little and the King saw what was ahead of him. A mass of black smouldering slime, bubbling from the intensity of the deadly dragon's fire.

The King took in a deep breath and stretched the bow strings a little tighter.

Before the King could release the arrow, the Bad hit Gerth dead centre in the belly with a huge tentacle knocking the dragon to one side. The King lost his grip and fell off the dragon. He was twisting in mid air. All five dragons immediately flew as fast as they could to try and catch the King. Everyone on the ground looked up. Their faces showing desperation. Everything was happening so fast!

33

The King felt himself roll as he was falling.

Now facing the fast approaching blob, if he could do anything he would hit it dead in the centre, for he could do nothing else. By pure chance when he was thrown off the dragon, he kept a tight hold onto the bow and arrow. The arrow was now back on the strings.

The King pulled the bow strings as far back as possible, hearing the creaks and moans of tension coming from the weapon. Without a second thought or hesitation, he let go of the string and saw the arrow fly. Time seemed to slow down. He saw the arrow release in such a gentle fashion, that it never quivered when it left the strings of the bow. It simply flew in a perfect straight line.

The King now waited for his own fate.

For those final seconds of his fall he shouted, "Die. Die. DIE!"

The arrow plunged into the black blob and the whole of its body caved in from the centre, like it was being sucked from the inside. At the same time the King prepared himself for his own death. He closed his eyes and silently praised all the braves souls that he had fought side by side with. He waited for his death.

A dragon caught him in one of its massive claws and whisked him away only feet from death. The King quickly opened his eyes and looked at the black mass. Its centre constantly imploding until it started to shudder. Small holes started to appear from the half caved in body, and everyone saw beams of different coloured light burst forth from the slime. The light show was eating the Bad from the inside. Small explosions could be seen followed by more streams of light escaping.

Everyone retreated to a safer distance, and the King was gently put back on the ground with the five dragons landing close to him.

The Bad was making noises of pain. It vibrated, paused, then exploded sending its slimy black and brown waste everywhere.

Instead of covering everyone in black goo, the black stuff evaporated in mid air leaving just the blue sky to shine upon the army. Except for one little bit, which continued to fall from the sky until it hit the ground.

The King, Elder Perennial Swallowtail, some of the faeries as well as the dragons and other mythical creatures looked at what had hit the ground.

A small crater had appeared in the ground, and in the centre of the crater was a small amount of the Bad. No bigger than a shoe. The centre of the thing moved up and down as if it was breathing.

Gerth said, "Everyone move back, while I and my dragons incinerate it with fire."

All the dragons blasted it with their fire. For all who stood and watched, to their utter amazement the thing still lived.

Elder Swallowtail flew over and examined it. He came to the conclusion that it must be the source of the black mass, in other words.

"Pure evil," he said, "I think I know what it is and where it came from."

The King looked at the faery, "Whatever you know, please tell us."

Elder Swallowtail reached far into his mind and told them of what he knew about a man called Cassava.

"There was a soothsayer by the name of Cassava Oxalic Solari. He was obsessed with wanting to learn the properties of shape shifting. He thought if he could learn this skill, then he would be able to shape shift into a new body and eventually cheat death. He knew about brags and wanted their gift. He would do anything to get it.

After many years of studying and months of searching, he finally found a brag."

Everyone saw on Elder Swallowtail's face that he seemed distressed.

"Take your time my friend," Gerth gently said.

With a sigh the faery gathered his thoughts and continued with the story.

"One very dark night a goblin had undressed itself and transformed into a wolf. You see, a brag can only transform back to its original form once it has returned to pick up its own clothes. This little secret is what Cassava knew.

He had tracked down a brag and watched it transform. As soon as the transformed brag had left, Cassava quickly grabbed the clothes and off he went to a place that he thought would guarantee him his gift of shape shifting. To the top of a mountain called Great End in the great lakes.

Eventually he made it to the summit of Great End. He could also sense the brag was chasing him after it had found out its clothes had been taken.

A few days before this incident, Cassava had gathered and taken a stack of wood to the top of the summit and constructed a table made from piled up rocks. That night on top of the mountain, he pulled out from under his cloak a goatskin water container containing something special. Suddenly the brag appeared. It was ready to leap and kill him. Cassava stood there holding the clothes in his right hand, which he held over the burning wood he had lit. The brag backed off, knowing only to well what would happen if the clothes were destroyed. It also knew what was in the goatskin container.

Blood from a wolf and some of Cassava's own blood. You see, Cassava thought that mixing his own blood with the blood of the animal that the brag had transformed into, would give him the power to shape shift. He didn't know that the brag had the power to call upon help, and it did.

Cassava was about to pour the blood mixture onto the clothes so he could throw everything onto the fire, when shadows the brag called upon appeared. These shadows grabbed and held Cassava still. He couldn't move.

The brag retrieved its clothes and transformed back into its own form. It walked towards Cassava telling him that he could have the power to transform. The brag mixed it's own blood with the blood in the container and poured it over Cassava.

He started to melt, as a thick oily black liquid oozed out of the container covering him from head to toe. What was left of Cassava was a pool of black liquid. Oily to the touch.

It was gathered up and the brag carried the soulless creature to the edge of a lake. With no hesitation the brag threw the creature into the lake and left it to a watery grave.

My thoughts on this are, the thing that I am convinced is Cassava must of lived and slowly grew to what we have all faced in battle. Sadly, this here what we see is what is left of Cassava now."

One of the goblins that listened to the story nodded and looked at the ground with shame.

"Do not feel you have done wrong," the King spoke softly to the goblin.

"We are all part of this and we all must deal with it. You and your kind have fought bravely."

Gerth said, "If our fire cannot kill it, what can we do?"

A faery came and approached Elder Swallowtail. He was dressed in a tanned leather top, each arm housed three beautifully crafted knives with Celtic designs along the blades and handles. A large belt was worn from the left shoulder across the chest and down to the right hip. This helped to carry a sword made of silver, which was housed upright on the back of the faery. He was also wearing dark green boots, black and tanned leather trousers and covered by a dark green mossy clock.

Looking at Elder Swallowtail he said, "Forgive me Sire, but can we not use the stone circle?"

Elder Swallowtail smiled at the faery, "My faithful and brave friend, Ash Skullcap," he placed a hand on his shoulder.

"As a protector of the five elements your heart is in the right place and your idea is sound, but I feel for the human, Cassava. Given time I may find away to free him from the form he is now."

Elder Swallowtail knew he should destroy the beast completely, but in his heart he felt he should show compassion and try to find away to reverse the curse the brags placed on Cassava.

The King stepped closer to it putting a hand on the neck of Gerth, patting him.

"We must put a spell on it."

Gerth bent down looking at the King, "What spell?"

"A spell that will not be broken. A spell made by all of us." the King replied.

"A spell of myths, legends and folklore," Elder Swallowtail

said.

All of the mythical creatures and the Kings army came together at the outer rim of Birchover wood. The King and those who represented the myths, legends and folklore met inside it.

They all stood in the centre of a large circle, and in the middle was placed the ingredients of the spell.

The King gave his shield representing him and his country. The faeries brought forth an assortment of herbs, in which they wrapped the Bad in and tied it up with spiders silk. The goblins spoke words that no-one but their own could understand. From their mouths a cold mist covered the wrapped up Bad, and the dragons breathed gently a blue flame from their nostrils that sealed everything up.

They placed the entombed monster onto the king's shield. The shield then slowly wrapped itself around the package creating a strong prison.

The whole package that represented the myths, legends and folklore was then buried deep within the wood of Birchover.

To seal the package and keep it imprisoned completely, one seed from an oak tree was planted on top of it to keep it from escaping. Elder Swallowtail uttered some words and the seed grew into an adult oak tree. Its roots enclosed itself around the package like an impenetrable cage, deep down in the earth.

5

- MYTHS, LEGENDS & FOLKLORE'S CELEBRATION -

After the victory, all the King's soldiers and the mythical creatures celebrated the victory with a banquet that lasted three days. Everything was back to normal with the Bad vanquished.

The King stood up and spoke to the victorious.

"My friends," everyone went quiet, "we have stood on the verge of defeat. Faced a terrible enemy that seemed to be invincible. In the end, all things that are good prevailed. It is the goodness that should be honoured here today."

The King picked up his cup and shouted, "TO GOODNESS!" and drank from his goblet followed by everyone else.

"Now that the thing is being held imprisoned, let our beliefs in one another keep the spell strong. Never forget each other. Always protect one another and be in peace."

From that time on, England continued to prosper and the tale of the great battle was written down in books for everyone to read, told by generations after the King had died.

The last remaining bit of the Bad remained buried deep within the earth, trapped by an oak tree. It lay quiet and undisturbed. Held by a magic that could only be broken, if humans were to forget that mythical creatures were true and all around us.

As time went on the stories became just that, stories told to keep children from misbehaving. A story to give a child exciting dreams before the morning sun rose in the sky. As the stories were changed, the magic of the spell became that little bit weaker. The creatures that were true and alive were now forgotten and thought of as mere stories. Nothing like those creatures could ever be true.

The time of magic was fading, and now a new age was being accepted slowly. Science was the new magic.

There were some who still believed. Like the old woman who lived in the wood. Or the travellers that went from village to village. But these people were few in numbers and not enough to keep the magic strong. They knew with a heavy heart that one day, the Bad would be back.

6

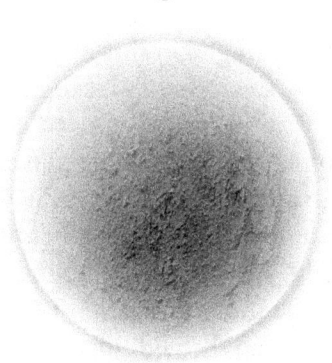

- FESTIVE CELEBRATIONS -
- OUR TIME -

A full moon was shining with a brilliance unmatched for as long as anyone could remember, surrounded by stars that seemed to bring movement to the night sky. Deep down in the wood where blackness was plentiful, there was a stir. Something was happening that mere mortal man had not witnessed for a millennium.

As the tree tops were illuminated by the glow of the moon, down at the base of the trees a different kind of light was active. A light show. A magnitude of colour was dancing, flying, gliding around the trees. A beautiful melodious sound as if Earth was singing to the trees and they were singing back. The lights zigzagged shooting here, there and everywhere in all directions. The activity was fast and graceful, only matched by the beautiful sound of song.

Where the trees were standing and the dancing lights were

moving, there was an area where a circle had been formed. Some trees made up the boundary around the circle. About fifty feet wide, all the activity was staged in this circle. As the light was moving shapes could be seen. Small, large, thin and obese shapes were all moving in rhythm with colours and sounds. Blues, reds, purples, greens and pinks were all dancing. Some were tiny spots of light no bigger than a thumb nail. Some as big as a man's hand.

Occasionally, a ball of light would glow and grow till it was the size of a small child. The image of the creature making the light was not seen for the glow concealed its inner beauty.

The creature flew up through the trees, zigzagging among the branches so not to hit them, knowing that the branches themselves would move away before any damage could be done.

Through the canopy of the trees it broke through, reaching high in the night sky trying to touch the beacon of light that was the moon. It stopped and floated on the slight breeze that was in the air. It starred looking ahead.

The countryside was dark but its shape still recognisable. The purity of the land had not yet been spoilt by man. Those feelings it felt sent an excitement through the creature's heart, and it danced once more making shapes of light and glowed more intense in the night air. The creature of light changed its size and was now the size of an apple. Falling back to earth into the thicket of trees, the little creature joined the procession that was celebrating with the moon.

This magical time was happening for a reason. A celebration of good times and freedom, as well as a celebration of victory. The joy of the friendships that were made, and the continuing imprisonment of the Bad under the oldest tree in the wood. A spell of myth, folklore and human magic holding it secure.

The creatures celebrated, and remembered the time when man and creatures of the wood mixed with each other, helping one another with all things. When myths, legends and folklore were believed by every living soul. From young suckling child to elderly grandparents. From big brother to little sister, and from mother to daughter, father to son. Men, women and children once knew all about the creatures of the wood, and the creatures of the wood knew about them.

As time passed by, the creatures of the wood still remembered mankind but mankind slowly forgot about them. Only remembering them as stories told to little children. Written down in books telling the tales of hobgoblins, dragons, dryads, ogres, and gnomes just to name a few. Choosing to believe in man made science rather than nature's magic.

If only mankind would remember. He would know that the stuff of myths and legends were not mere tales of wild imaginative story tellers, but they are in fact tales of truth that the creatures did live and still do. Still living in the woods today, still remembering the time when man and mythical creature lived together in harmony.

In the wood, the mythical creatures called faeries were flying shedding their magical light around the circle of trees, bringing light into a place that would normally be dark. The outlines of creatures dancing were having a wonderful time.

Clapping and swaying. Gnomes, derricks, dobbies and oakmen were all mixing together like brothers and sisters. On the shoulder of some of these creatures were portunes, a tiny farming spirit only half an inch in height. There were more creatures on this night than had been in a long long time. All living things were happy. All were remembering the good times and not thinking about the bad times

On a branch overlooking the party of light and song, was a faery that did not take much notice of the celebration. She was looking over the trees and in the direction of the tree that held the Bad. She was troubling her mind with the question, "*What if?*"

It seemed a question that her people had not considered for some time.

"*What if the Bad escaped? What if the Bad was to gain strength? What if the myths are totally forgotten?*" the little faery kept asking herself over and over again.

The little creature just looked in the direction of the tree that held the Bad, ignoring the procession below.

At the foot of the tree another faery was darting around

looking for someone. Shining the colour of green grass this creature shone brightly. His tiny wings flapped a thousand beats a minute, only making a slight humming sound as he flew. He had a fine physique, which matched his healthy spirit for living.

He darted over to his best friend who was humming in tune with the music, "Balamore!" he shouted. His friend couldn't hear him.

"BALAMORE!" this time he got his friends attention.

"ZEAL!" Balamore's face shone brighter when he saw his good friend fly over.

"Zeal. Great to see you."

Zeal smiled and asked his friend, "Balamore, have you seen Caitlin?"

Balamore kept switching his eyes from the dancing colours of his friends, to Zeal.

"Zeal, all you need to do is look up to the stars and you will see."

Zeal looking at his friend saw that he was pointing upwards. Both looked and could see a small faint light of gold, not moving but bright enough to know that Caitlin was sitting on a branch.

"Go to her. Drag her to the dance," Balamore said.

"Easier said than done," Zeal replied.

"What have you done now, Zeal?" Balamore laughed out loud, "You didn't shower her with gooseberry juice again, did you?"

"It wasn't gooseberry. It was raspberry juice and no, I haven't sprayed her with anything, not yet anyway," a cheeky grin appeared on Zeal's face.

"Well, what are you waiting for? Go to her. Get her down from the trees. She'll listen to you."

Zeal smiled at his friend, Balamore Skullcap. Balamore was more of a brother than a friend to him. They were inseparable. The two of them would do anything for each other.

Zeal looked up and off he flew to the golden light that was perched on a branch.

Caitlin was looking out in the direction of the tree that held the Bad imprisoned, when Zeal flew up. Hardly making a noise he thought he would surprise her, but she knew it was him.

"Hey! Caitlin."

She looked at him and smiled. Her golden colour was shining, but not like how Zeal knew it could shine.

"Zeal, it's nice to see you. Are you having a good time?" Caitlin asked him.

Zeal fluttered around Caitlin, "GREAT TIME!" he proudly shouted, listening to the words as they echoed through the night sky.

"Why don't you come down and dance? The elders would love to hear you sing."

Caitlin smiled and looked away.

Zeal's tone of voice softened as he spoke, "What's wrong Caitlin?"

"Huh, is no one concerned about the tree?" Caitlin asked Zeal.

"Am I the only one who is noticing changes in the air?"

Zeal couldn't see why she was concerning herself with a thing such as a tree, especially the one that the Bad was imprisoned under. But he thought he would go along with it.

"Caitlin, you can't stay up here all the time. Just come with me and have at least a bit of a good time," Zeal said.

Caitlin looked back at Zeal and saw in his eyes that he really wanted her to enjoy herself.

"You still haven't got me back for the raspberry soaking I did on you last week," Zeal knew that would get Caitlin smiling.

Zeal was right. Caitlin could not help but smile from ear to ear. She loved Zeal a lot. Caitlin looked at the moon and said to it. "Keep shining. Keep protecting. And keep a watch on the tree."

She jumped up taking hold of Zeal's hand, and the two flew down to the party below.

As the party was in high spirits and cheeriness, no one was taking any notice of what was happening deeper in the wood, where the oldest of the trees stood. Caitlin was right in feeling worried about the Bad escaping. She knew that one day it would.

All those years ago, when man and myth conjured up a

very powerful spell to hold the Bad under the tree, the strength of the spell lay in the fact that everyone and everything would live together and help each other.

As the years had passed, and more of man forgot about the creatures of the wood, the spell that held the Bad captive began to weaken. The spell would have been broken long before now if it wasn't for the stories that mankind told, keeping a glimmer of hope alive.

The oakmen of the wood made sure that the old oak tree was never touched. Mankind had an irresistible taste for advancement, and if that meant that a tree, a wood or a whole piece of countryside had to be ripped out and bulldozed over, then so be it.

Thankfully, this woodland was safe, protected by mankind himself. It was protected by the Forestry Commission and could not be used for anything, except for ramblers and the odd family having a picnic. The woodland and the surrounding countryside was safe.

The old oak tree stood majestically tall and proud. Proud that it had outlived most things. The bright moon showered the tree with its glistening silver light, and the leaves of the tree gladly accepted the silver coverage. There was a slow moving breeze in the air that caressed every leaf on the tree. It looked like the whole tree was dancing to the music that the faeries were making at the circle.

Every creature of the wood loved the tree and treated it with the utmost respect. It was home for a whole host of creatures such as, squirrels, blue tits, the odd red robin and an assortment of insects. It was sanctuary as well as a burial ground for those that had breathed their final breath.

Many a bird or land animal would come to the base of the tree to live out their final moments. As their life was drawing to a close, the tree would gently shake sending down a quilt of leaves, a gesture of farewell to an animal of the wood. The tree was the symbol of the wood. Long living and a home for all who came to it.

No one could hear what was happening at the base of the tree. A low muffled sound started from deep down, deep under the ground. Then there was a slight vibration, enough to send a few leaves scattering from the long extended arms of the branches. Next came a hissing noise, only a whisper but that was all that was needed. And then lastly, a slight rumble of the ground occurred at the base of the tree. No one was watching or could hear anything.

The chain of events settled down as if nothing had happened. Trouble always starts small.

After everything had quietened down, no one would notice that there had appeared a slight crack at the very base of the tree. The crack was not very big, a few inches long and an inch wide, that was all that was needed. The Bad would now wait. It had waited for a thousand years. A little while longer would not hurt. Time was on its side.

The celebrations were still going strong and Caitlin decided to sing. To lift herself out of the droopy mood she was in, she decided to sing a song of hope and happiness.

Everyone knew she had a beautiful voice and when she sang, her golden light would always light up the surrounding area. In fact, it was known that when a human child enters the woodland and loses direction, Caitlin would scurry off towards the lost child and sing, gaining the attention of the child. The child would immediately see the glow of Caitlin's aura, and she would lead the child out of the wood to safety. Of course when the child got home and told his or her parents, the parents would just laugh and accept it as the wild imagination of a young child. It was Caitlin's nature to help. She was never told to stop, for faeries to do such a thing was an honour and in their very nature.

The introduction started. One of the elder faeries flew to the centre of the circle. His wings beating slowly, a glow of brilliant white light surrounded him. Elder Dandelion Green Leaf was brimming with a smile. He was getting on a bit but still fit for his age and he had the utmost respect by everyone in the faery order.

For this occasion he was wearing a yellowish white robe. He was covered by a cloak that seemed to have every colour of green covering it, which seemed to mingle into each other as he moved about. On his head he wore a dandelion petal, which had strands of his hair braided in between the the strands of the petal.

He took a deep breath and gave everyone in the audience a quick glance, "Faeries. Ghouls. Oakmen, and alike. I would like to introduce to you the most enchanting voice of the wood. May all of you feel bewitched when you hear the sound of Caitlin, the golden light of the wood."

Elder Dandelion Green Leaf raised an arm in the direction of Caitlin. She fluttered over and hovered on a spot where everyone could see her. She clasped her hands together and sang a song of hope and happiness.

"The forest is singing as the wind flows through the leaves."
"The boughs they are swaying with the greatest of ease."
"As the birds are singing their melodious songs, truly Mother Nature is there to help all things along."

When she started to sing, it was like everything and everyone was suspended in time. The sound of her voice captivated all in attendance. As her voice flowed from her vocal chords, like a mist the words and the music flowed around each of the creatures who were listening. It was captivating and angelic, even the trees seemed to sway to the direction of the sound, drawing them closer to every note that was uttered.

"The hope and happiness that is felt in the air, well it's old Mother Nature saying we should never despair."
"Just look all around at the beauty we see."
"This will give hope to us all in a world that lacks peace."
"So happiness is part of all that is around, if only we would use it for the greater love of all that is to be found."

Her body expressed itself to every note that was released, and the sound seemed to rise higher and higher into the air and beyond the trees. Badgers, foxes, deer and squirrels could not help but be captured by the glory of the sound.

As Caitlin's voice increased in pitch, her aura shone brighter and brighter. Her voice would bring peace to any situation and could tame any animal.

She fluttered among the four legged animals touching them, caressing their fur as she reached a point in her song. She flew back to the centre of the circle preparing herself for the finale.

"Now happiness is part of all that is with us. If only we would use it, love that is sound."
"For life it runs along, side by side. With all dreams coming true and friendships build up."
"To make them strong and true."

"Hope and happiness there for the taking, open your eyes and let life be yours true."
"Hope and happiness there for the taking, open your eyes and let life be yours true."

She got to the last few words and raised her arms high above her head pointing to the moon. The last word left her lips, and her ever glowing colour of gold burst up from her and into the sky. A magical display of fireworks shooting into space, spreading colour into the night sky then slowly falling back to earth.

Gradually her colour dimmed and everyone and everything saw her with her arms folded around her thin, delicate body and her face looking to the ground.

The whole place erupted in a chorus of excitement. Deer making deep throated sounds and swaying their heads. Badgers stamping on the ground disturbing the lose soil. Squirrels running frantically up and down branches and jumping over one another. The foxes were making a barking type sound, raising their heads and looking into the night sky. Some owls had joined the cheering crowd making a drawn out screeching noise and twisting their heads in glee.

Caitlin was embarrassed by the eruption of excitement. Her natural glow of golden light was throbbing.

Elder Dandelion Green Leaf came over and placed his arms around her, "Well done. Well done my dear."

Her uncontrollable smile was infectious.

Always a delight to hear your voice," Elder Dandelion Green Leaf said to her.

Caitlin flew off and floated next to Zeal and Balamore. There she tried to hide her embarrassment.

As Elder Green Leaf flew back to the edge of the circle the delights of the crowd died down. A very elderly faery came to the centre of the circle. Gliding across the floor his wings beating slowly. So slowly you could almost count the beats.

He was dressed in an autumn brown cloak, had long white strands of hair braided in long lengths reaching down to his ankles. The ends of the braided hair flowed freely, catching every whiff of air moving as if they were fingers trying to catch an insect.

He was called Elder Perennial Swallowtail. His light was silver, and he had great knowledge of all things good as well as a master of spell casting, and just like the meaning of Perennial, no one really knew how old he was.

Tonight was not only a celebration of goodness, but of the beginning of Spring. A time of newness for the countryside, and a new carpet of colour would spring forth across the wood.

Elder Perennial Swallowtail stopped as he reached the centre of the circle and so did his wings. Everything about him was perfectly still. Instead of falling to the ground he just hung in mid air, motionless.

The crowd looked on with anticipation. Then they were rewarded. Everyone saw Elder Swallowtail had a smile on his face. Looking at them he addressed the crowd.

He spoke in a voice that sounded as ancient as the trees and as gentle as a cool summer breeze.

"It is my privilege and honour to bestow upon the woodland a gift."

Every creature watching stood with their breath held in

50

tight.

"A gift that will ensure the protection of all who live here and a symbol of friendship to all who visit our home."

Elder Perennial Swallowtail's voice floated through the air, having the effect like he was personally speaking to each and everything at the circle.

The aura of silver that surrounded Elder Swallowtail exploded into a light as bright as a star. From beneath him, silver speckles of light poured like a thunderous waterfall down to the ground, covering and expanding across the floor of the circle.

From the silver light shot four beams travelling in different directions. Each beam hitting a tree. The four trees glowed silver, every bit of bark, trunk, branch and leaf. On the ground the silver particles of light covered the floor like a sheet of silvery coloured ice.

Everyone took in gulps of air mesmerised by the spectacle.

The four beams of light stopped and the silver particles of light gently disappeared. What was left was no less amazing.

The trees that were covered with the silver light were now covered in flowers of different colours. The branches sprouted new buds of blue, silver, yellow and purple flowers. As each branch touched another tree, so that tree started to shoot new buds that bloomed in full colour.

As for the magic on the floor, the same thing happened only the flowers in bloom were of different sizes and varieties. Around the edges of the trees sprouted daffodils, white and yellow. On the woodland floor, bluebells, pink purslane, red campion, foxglove and rhododendrons. The wood became a carpet of colour, a master piece of nature.

All the living creatures just looked in admiration, and Elder Perennial Swallowtail's cloak was now silver in colour. Holding a smile, he fluttered down to one of the daffodils and touched it. The touch made the daffodil and all the other flowers colours radiate even more. Every creature in the wood was happy.

After that, more magical creatures joined the celebration, and the music and magic continued until the moon moved on and its sister the sun took over. As the sun started to rise all the animals departed and went their own separate ways.

The owls went to the trees, the foxes back to their dens, the deer went to the fields and the badgers went deeper into the wood. As for the faeries, ghouls, oakmen and those that man has not seen in a lifetime, they gently disappeared back into the magic that keeps them away from us.

After the celebration and most of the animals had gone, Sup Sup Rose, a faery that loved to keep an eye out for injured animals or help those who are ready to give birth flew to the centre of the circle.

Looking at the morning sky, he saw it was bright with a few greyish clouds passing overhead. Sup Sup Rose flew to the top of the trees and peered further a field. In the distance he could see something was coming, it looked like a thunderstorm. Nodding to himself he knew a very bad storm was on its way.

"A good y'old soak wunt ert anythin," he whispered to himself.

Caitlin flew over to him, "How is it?" she asked.

Sup Sup kept his eyes on the sky, "Should pass. Now't orry about."

His gaze fixed firmly on the sky. After he was finished he looked at Caitlin in a more caring way, "Can't stop ear. Must see to those that eed me."

Caitlin loved Sup Sup Rose's attitude. One of caring and unselfishness. He couldn't speak very well, but what he could not do with words he made up with the attention he gave to the animals. He strongly believed that everything had a symbiotic relationship, and he felt passionately that he would do all he could to preserve that and help those in need, animal or human.

"Give my love to the animals, Sup Sup," Caitlin said to him.

He smiled and Caitlin kissed him on the cheek. His aura of rose pink throbbed for a second, then he flew away. Caitlin chuckled.

She leapt into the air, flying gracefully around trees skimming the soil of the woodland floor and leaving a wave of fallen leaves behind her. She then shot straight up until she came to a hole in a tree. Without hesitation she flew into the hole and inside the tree. Deep inside was her family of three brothers, seven sisters her mother and father. It was time for sleep.

- MOVING HOUSE -

"**M**um! I hate moving house," a voice came shouting from upstairs, as he was placing the last of his books into a cardboard box. The boy's mother came from the other bedroom and in to his sitting down next to him.

"You've never moved house before," shaking her head from side to side smiling at her son's comments.

"Solomon, it will be much better for your health."

His mother placed a hand on his head and stroked his thick blanket of auburn hair. She bent down and kissed his cheeks, stood up and walked to the bedroom door.

"I'm going downstairs to make some sandwiches for the journey. When you've finished come down," Solomon nodded enthusiastically.

"Oh, Mum," Solomon said.

"Yes." Sarah answered

"Where has Dad gone?"

"He's just gone to have the car cleaned," she looked at Solomon hoping that the move would be the right thing to do.

After a short while Solomon came trotting down the stairs feeling that his stomach needed feeding, and his daily routine of popping down a million pills was needed to be done.

Sarah and Dave Larch were two people who, like many other couples had tried having a child for some time. They got married in their early twenties, having known each other since they were seven years old.

They grew up together, going to the same school and being in the same class, always helping one another with school work and alike. Friends described them as inseparable, funny and always there if you needed a friend. Both graduated with excellent grades and Dave went on to study graphic design. Sarah went on to study art. She graduated from University with a Masters Degree in Fine Arts and after graduating, she taught art at a local night school.

Dave and Sarah loved each other very much. After Dave got a good job at a prominent design house, he and Sarah saved up enough money to get married and buy a house near the centre of Manchester

For five years, Dave made a name for himself as a dedicated, talented and reliable designer. He could think up ideas on the spare of the moment that were both visually easy to understand, and most importantly were workable ideas.

For four of those five years Dave and Sarah had been trying to have a child, with no success and had consulted specialists on what was the reason. In the end they had tried everything except surgery.

One Saturday morning when Dave was finishing up on a design, he received a phone call from Sarah. She was screaming down the phone. Not a scream of fright but a scream of delight. Shouting, laughing as she was trying to tell Dave something.

"Sarah! Sarah!" Dave was shouting back. "What's the matter? What's going on?" he was confused by the vibes of excitement he was getting from Sarah.

"Dave," she said, "are you sitting down?"

Dave looked at his legs and said, "Er, yes."

Sarah took a deep breath and said in one long slow voice, "David Samuel Larch. I'm pregnant."

It didn't take Dave more than 40 minutes to get home. Rush through the front door and into the arms of Sarah, who had been crying by the looks of the water marks that had slid down the sides of her cheeks.

The two of them went to bed early that evening. Cuddling up to each other and talking about the possibilities of it being a girl or boy.

First thing Monday morning, after Dave kissed Sarah goodbye and left for work, Sarah went off to the clinic. She eventually got to see the doctor just to confirm the pregnancy.

After a consultation Sarah had to have a blood test. The doctor told Sarah that the results will be at the clinic within the day, and she should could go home rest and wait for a call. Sarah waited and waited at home for about three hours, until the phone rang.

It was Dave, "Hi Sarah. Well!"

Sarah told him what had happened at the doctors and that she should wait for a call. After they both said goodbye Sarah put the phone down, then it rang again. She quickly picked it up and the clinic asked her to come round.

Sarah sat down on a chair in the doctors office and waited for the result. After speaking to Sarah for a few moments, the doctor finished the conversation by saying, "Mrs Larch, I would like to say congratulations. You are going to have a baby."

The shock hit Sarah and she simply burst out into tears. She rushed home and called Dave.

After slumping down on his office chair and putting the phone down. Dave screamed out, "YES!"

Everyone in the office turned round and stared at him.

Dave came back home with a huge bouquet of flowers. He and Sarah couldn't believe that it had actually happened. After so long. They were finally going to become parents.

Nine months later Dave was holding his new born son in his arms. Looking at his son, Dave whispered, "Welcome to the world Solomon."

Sarah smiled feeling very tired. A week later Sarah was finally told she could go home. The pregnancy had taken it out of her and Dave was being the perfect husband and now father.

Solomon Edward Larch grew fast and was a handful. He

proved to be a very inquisitive little boy. Once Solomon learnt to crawl, every time he would see his own reflection in a mirror he would crawl as fast as he could towards his reflection. Not knowing how to stop he would go crashing into the mirror, bouncing off and landing on his chubby bottom. Instead of crying, Solomon would just giggle trying to grab the kid in the mirror that looked like him.

Another time when he was beginning to walk, he found his way into the garage where his father was doing some work on the car. Dave saw him and said, "Hey, Solomon. Have you come to help me?"

Solomon just smiled and walked away. Dave put his head back under the bonnet of the car and thought nothing of it. He then heard a noise and jumped away from what he was doing. Dave saw what made the noise. It was Solomon, holding an empty bottle of new engine oil and dripping from head to toe in it. He just stood there giggling. Dave was relieved that nothing serious had happened.

During the years, Dave and Sarah had noticed that Solomon's health had deteriorated. He seemed to fall ill often. Often out of breath and sweating.

After speaking to a doctor they were told that due to pollution, Solomon, as well as many other children his age and older were suffering from Pulmonary Capacity. This meant a reduction in lung capacity because of the pollution in the air. This was frightening to Dave and Sarah, and after much careful thought they both decided to move.

A positive plan was needed and they both decided somewhere that was going to be good for Solomon's health, and a place that they could get to work from.

Finding the right place to move to was taking forever to find. Either the house was too far or too costly to buy, but the two of them were determined to move.

After about eight months of searching and a few days after Solomon's eighth birthday, Dave scoured the Internet Estate Agents for the hundredth time and came across a place of interest.

Sarah was watching Emmerdale farm the British soap opera

that she never missed. The end credits began to roll and Dave shouted her over to the computer, "I think I've found something."

Sarah came walking over and looked at the picture of a village in Derbyshire. Solomon came over holding Rupert the Bear in his arms and wanting to sit on his father's lap.

"Where is it, Dad?" Solomon asked as he was staring at the pictures of houses.

Dave held Solomon with one arm around his waist for safety, "A place called Birchover, Derbyshire."

"Where's Birchover?"

Sarah sensing a hundred questions were coming, grabbed Solomon from Dave's knee.

"Time for bed," she said, "the questions can continue tomorrow."

Without a moan or a groan, Solomon said good night to his Dad. Kissed him and ran upstairs followed by his mother. Solomon was never difficult when it came to going to bed.

After brushing his teeth and washing his face, he jumped into bed with Rupert next to him and snuggled down for the night. Sarah kissed Solomon and said, "Love you."

Looking at his mum with a big smile, Solomon said, "Love you too, Mum." It wasn't long before he fell into snoozy land.

Sarah came down to where Dave was and wrapped her arms around his neck, giving him a big kiss on his cheek, "So, what's this place?" Sarah asked.

"Birchover," Dave answered.

"Birchover?" she repeated.

The two of them sat in front of the screen. Dave explained that he thought it would be a great place to visit and see what the houses where like.

For a few weeks Sarah, Dave and Solomon visited Birchover a number of times. Looking at houses, schools and the surrounding countryside. The place was beautiful with walks of unmistakable beauty, and cottages that would normally be seen on the canvas of an oil painting.

After coming back home from their third outing to Birchover, Sarah took Solomon to bed. After she came down she and Dave talked about it.

"Well, what do you think?" Dave asked.

Sarah knew he loved it, but she was a little apprehensive about the move due to work commitments.

"I love the place Dave,"

"But," Dave interrupted. He knew what she was thinking.

"But...But what about our jobs? Especially yours."

"Sarah, remember Solomon and his problem? If we don't do it now we'll never do it."

"I know, I know, but what do we do for work? It's not like there are jobs in the village."

Sarah had a point, but Dave had been thinking about this for the last eight months. He would have to sound convincing if they were to move far enough from Manchester, but close enough to still be making a living.

"I've already been thinking about that," Dave answered.

He started to explain that he could easily work from home. His boss had been mentioning that as a way to keep costs down and keep people in work. The majority of work was done on computer and for Dave, it was mostly done at home. The only times Dave needed to be at work would be to go over ideas with clients, and then look at the final proofs once a job was ready to be finished.

Sarah listened and agreed that for Dave's situation it would work. For her it would be different. She posed the question, "How can I travel to and fro from Birchover to Manchester, and back again everyday? It would be impossible."

Dave had also thought about it and said to her, "Pack up your job."

Sarah's face dropped. She couldn't believe what he had just said.

"Are you insane?" she said.

From the look on her face Dave knew she didn't fully understand what he meant.

"Now, just listen."

He went on to tell her that her dream of teaching privately could come true. By dropping her teaching at night school, which didn't pay a lot anyway, she could concentrate on creating her own program of teaching. Invite paying students wanting to have a teaching course on their subject.

The Birchover scenery was ideal, tranquil and magical. The perfect canvas for students. The idea that Dave presented to Sarah was credible, and it would allow her to be with Solomon in the evenings more, as well as teach him how to paint and appreciate art.

"Okay," Sarah said, "Can I think about it? Let me weigh up a few things before I say yay or nay?"

Dave nodded and understood her enough to know that she would certainly think about it carefully, and if it was a viable idea she would say yes.

It took less than a week for Sarah to say 'Yes,' to Dave. Now all that was needed was to find that special home. They looked extensively at estate agents and after about two more months of soul searching, they found the house they wanted.

They didn't find it hard to sell their own home, and shortly after they had signed the contracts for their new house in Birchover, it was time to say goodbye to their old life in the city of Manchester. A city that had once been grotty, now Manchester was a thriving city of business and fashion.

Dave came back after taking the car for a clean, and walked into the house for the last time. He held a rose in his hand for Sarah and for Solomon, he had the 2010 edition of Rupert the Bear. Solomon couldn't get it at the time, and when he saw it he was thrilled.
Looking at his son, Dave said, "Now, all your Rupert books are up to date."

Solomon gave his dad a big kiss and ran to the living room to have a good look through his new book.

"Where did you get that?" Sarah asked.

"I knew Solomon would be a bit moody moving, so I've had this on order for a few weeks. I thought it would cheer him up a bit."

Sarah loved Dave's timing. Thought it was lovingly cheeky. They carried the last few boxes out of the house and Sarah closed the front door for the last time. They got into the car, looked at the house they had lived in for twelve years and said goodbye to it. Solomon gave a hearty wave goodbye.

Dave put the car into gear and they drove away. The last thing they did before leaving Manchester was to drop off the door keys at the estate agents.

8

- WOODLAND MEETING -

It was the first week of Summer. All the animals of the wood were either looking after new members of their family, or awaiting the arrival of new ones.

The sun was shining and as usual it brought out the best of the flowers. The scents of the wild flowers were being carried on the summer breeze. Bees were buzzing around collecting nectar for the hives, and the occasional rambler was strolling through the wood keeping to the tracks designated for them.

The faeries had been busy by helping out with the birth of new ones among the badgers, deer, foxes and squirrels. Helping out by trying to ease the delivery process and limiting any complications. This was what faeries enjoyed doing, as well as overseeing the wild flowers and making sure that the smaller insects, like the bees and butterflies could collect enough nectar to survive on.

Summer was always a busy season no matter what kind of creature you were, and the busiest of all faeries was Sup Sup Rose.

Sup Sup Rose had gathered an assembly in the circle and had designated various faeries as heads of groups. Zeal White Oak for the deer. Balamore Skullcap for the badgers. Mugwort Ringworm for the foxes. Boomer Safflower for the hedgehogs, and

Yellow Dock for the squirrels.

Within the groups were at least six to ten other faeries, each helping out in case of emergencies. It was a well organised group that had gathered together. Caitlin had teamed up with Sup Sup Rose. They were off to a burrow where there was a group of rabbits waiting for new ones to be born. This group was of particular interest to Sup Sup Rose, because many years ago he had a terrible experience with a cat.

A domestic cat had come into the woods, which was very unusual for that type of animal. The cat saw Sup Sup Rose standing on a log. Creeping up slowly to the faery, the cat quickly swiped him off the log. He hit the ground hard damaging one of his wings. He was only able to fly short distances and close to the ground. The cat wanted to play with Sup Sup Rose before the inevitable.

Luckily, a rabbit saw what was happening to the faery. Sup Sup Rose's life was in terrible danger. The rabbit moved silently towards the cat. Before the cat could take another swipe at the faery, quick as a flash the rabbit jumped onto the back of the cat. It screeched with fright not knowing what had hit it. Before it could find out, Sup Sup Rose had grabbed the fur of the rabbit and the two of them fled as fast as they could go through the wood. The wounded faery held on for dear life.

The cat gave chase, but the rabbit knowing the wood was too nimble to be caught. Within a few moments, Sup Sup Rose and the rabbit were deep within the wood and the cat gave up the chase. In-fact, the cat was chased away by a passing fox that had picked up its scent. On that day the cat certainly lost one of its nine lives.

After Sup Sup Rose counted who was who at the gathering, and which group he or she was in, he ordered everyone to go and help the families out. The whole place lit up in to rainbow of colours as each group whizzed off to complete their assignments.

Sup Sup Rose looked at Caitlin and asked, "Are ye ready?" Caitlin's face shone brighter, "Ready," she said.

With excitement in his voice, Sup Sup Rose gave the order, "Then let's go."

He was taking Caitlin to the rabbit den that housed the family of the rabbit that saved his life. This was to be that rabbit's final chance of seeing his growing family. He was getting old and felt soon that it was time to go to the old tree and rest. There, he would wait for the leaves to cover him so that he could go back to the earth.

"Thank you so much, Sup Sup for this," Caitlin said, not able to hold her excitement.

"It's me pleasure," he answered, "Zeal mentioned tha yud like to see a mamily of rabbits give girth. Sorry, give birth."

Sometimes he felt embarrassed with the way he spoke, but only with strangers. His friends including Caitlin, Zeal and Balamore didn't care. They took him for who he was.

Both of them flew as fast as they could to get to the rabbit's den and to help out when they could. They both came across the rabbit hole, and was greeted by a small rabbit no more than six months old. The three of them dived into the hole the rabbit showing them the way. Right turn, left turn and right through a maze of tunnels. Finally the rabbit brought them to a large opening, and there in the centre surrounded by other rabbits was a mother ready to give birth.

The two angelic lights entered and lit up the whole burrow. Gold and pink colours covered the walls. A large rabbit came over and placed its nose onto the tiny hand of Sup Sup Rose. It was the rabbit that saved his life.

Sup Sup Rose knew what to do now and asked Caitlin to stay with his friend, the elder rabbit.

Sup Sup moved slowly to the female who was breathing hard, and he gently caressed her soft warm nose. This action seemed to help because it was calming the female rabbit down. Her breathing settled and it now had a more natural rhythm to it.

Once Sup Sup Rose was happy with everything his light of rose pink increased. He was happy with how things were going. The rabbit started to shuffle slightly, then her back legs appeared to move. Sup Sup flew over to his friend the rabbit and whispered something in to his ear. The rabbit moved over to the female and caressed her nose.

64

"What's happening?" Caitlin asked, she was mesmerised by what she was seeing.

In a whisper, Sup Sup said, "Our friend the rabbit, tis his great gran, gran, granddaughter who is giving birth. I told im to try and comfort her," never taking his eyes of the female rabbit who was now ready to give birth.

The two faeries were near to tears after they saw what they thought were the first signs of legs coming out into the world.

Sup Sup Rose saw that the female's breathing was getting a little erratic and quickly flew over.

He assessed the situation and started to glide his tiny hands down the soft fur belly of the female rabbit. More of the baby rabbit was being pushed out, and more soothing was the caressing touch of Sup Sup Rose's hands on the belly of the female. With one final push, a baby rabbit slipped out onto the ground and all the other rabbits quickly surrounded it, and started to lick and clean it so that the youngster could get it's first taste of fresh air.

Quickly, Sup Sup Rose gave the little one a quick going over and said that everything was great. During the whole session of delivering baby rabbits, nine were born.

"Tat's a healthy litter," he said, looking at all the youngsters huddled up to their mother. Caitlin was speechless after such an event.

After a while it was time to go. The whole litter of nine newly born bunny rabbits were doing well.

Sup Sup turned to Caitlin, "I'm going with my friend to the tree."

Caitlin knew why and didn't ask to go. It was between him and his old friend.

As Sup Sup Rose, Caitlin and the rabbit left the hole that led out of the burrow, Caitlin kissed the rabbit goodbye and flew away. Tears were falling from her eyes on to the fertile soil of the wood. Sup Sup Rose and the rabbit went off deeper into the wood looking for that final resting place.

It is a strange thing that when an animal knows it is time to pass on, other animals that would view it as food stay away. A last notion of respect. A way of saying, "You beat the odds. You lived till the end."

As the two travellers passed through the wood other animals looked on. A fox and a family of badgers all lowered their heads, their way of saying goodbye.

Sup Sup Rose kept stroking the rabbit but didn't say a word for the full length of the journey. Words would do nothing but a touch would say everything.

Finally, after a while the two gazed upon the tree that had been standing in the same spot since the beginning of time. They had arrived at the base of the old tree. The two companions faced each other. Tears were streaming down the face of Sup Sup Rose and the nose of the rabbit soaked them up.

"I...I will miss you so much, my old friend," Sup Sup Rose's voice breaking under the emotion of seeing his friend for the last time.

He placed his lips on the soft fur of the rabbits nose, and gently sprinkled some fine dust on the head of his friend.

"May this help you to dream on your journey to a better place."

He slowly backed up and the rabbit hopped to the base of the tree. Stumbling slightly but still having the strength to make it.

The rabbit turned around and looked back. They both looked at each other and the rabbit slowly lowered its body onto the soil. The rabbit moved a little to get a comfortable resting place. It then closed its eyes and Sup Sup Rose saw the belly of his friend stop moving. His friend had passed on.

Before Sup Sup Rose flew away he saw the tree shake a little. From the branches of the tree came a shower of summer leaves, gracefully falling ever so slowly and covering his friend the rabbit. He knew it was now over.

Sup Sup Rose was about to go, when he noticed something that he hadn't seen before. At the base of the tree was a dark line of some sort. He flew closer and touched the line. It was not a natural line normally caused by age, it was a deep crack that had not been there before.

His instincts went on high alert and he could feel the air around him go very cold.

"O...O...O..." A slight stutter stopped him from finishing his sentence.

"The spirit of the woodland. What has happened?"

He noticed that all around him there was no sound. No birds singing. No breeze in the air. Everything had gone quiet. Just then he heard a noise like a twig being snapped. Immediately, he fluttered his wings as fast as he could and zoomed off dodging every branch and twig by millimetres. He had to get back as fast as he could. He had to get back to the centre of the circle to tell the others what he had found.

Dave, Sarah and Solomon were on their way to Birchover. The drive to their new home was beautiful. Solomon looked mesmerized seeing all the green trees and wild flowers that were all in full bloom. He had never seen so many all at once. Both Dave and Sarah were feeling happy with themselves knowing their son will have a healthier life from now on.

Solomon was looking through the window of the car and screamed with excitement, "WOW!"

Sarah spun round to see her son, "What is it?" she asked.

Solomon couldn't take his eyes off the sight he saw, "Mum. Mum. Look!" he kept saying.

Sarah looked and saw what made Solomon excited.

A farmer was rounding up his flock of sheep using a black dog and whistling at the same time.

"I've read about this, Mum?" Solomon said.

Sarah laughed seeing how innocent things can seem to a young child.

"And now you are seeing it," she said to him, "how does it compare?"

Solomon looked serious at the scene before him, "It doesn't. It's amazing to see it."

Sarah smiled looking at her son, and as she turned around to face the front she herd Solomon silently say, "WOW!"

The whole journey took about an hour and a half. Halfway through the journey, Solomon needed to go to the toilet so it was a mad rush to find a place. In the end, Dave parked at the side of a quiet road so Solomon could run to a tree and do his thing. Eventually, they arrived at their new home.

The house looked beautiful. It may have been empty but it still had character. Dave picked up Solomon after giving him the front door key, and positioned him so that he could put the key in the keyhole. Solomon's hand was a bit shaky but he managed to get the key in.

"Come on lad," Dave mumbled under the strain, "You're a ton weight."

The key slid into the keyhole. Solomon turned the key and Sarah turned the doorknob. The door opened and Dave put his son down. Solomon ran into the house. His mum and dad followed holding each other's hands and wearing a huge smile.

They walked into the living room, which was empty and dusty. The first room looked magical with the dust swirling through the air, and light beaming through the gaps of the half closed curtains. It looked like a natural light show to welcome the new owners.

"What do you think, Solomon?" Dave asked.

"MAGIC!" Solomon shouted and everyone laughed.

The place did feel magical.

Outside at the front of the house, an old dry stone wall outlined the boundary of the front garden. It was covered with an assortment of flowers and colours that sang out to anyone who looked at them.

Solomon was running in and out of rooms shouting, "Magic! Magic!" He nearly fell tripping over his own footing. He looked back at where he nearly fell and saw something that was so small, that it would have been easy to miss, or sweep up with a brush without knowing it was there. What Solomon saw was a small garment. A dress of such infinite beauty that it shone or twinkled in the light from the sun.

He bent down and picked it up. Holding it in his hand he looked at it studiously. With a whisper of a voice he said,

"Beautiful."

The garment seemed to glow as he whispered the word. After a few seconds the glow faded.

"What do you have there, Solomon?" his mother asked.

He lifted up his hand and showed his mother. Sarah looked and poked it with her finger. It glistened. She thought it was the sun catching something silver in the garment.

"It must have been a dress for a very small doll," she said.

Solomon looked at his mum and asked, "Can I keep it, please?"

"Of course you can. Put it safely away so that you don't lose it."

Solomon placed it carefully in the front pocket of his baggy dungarees, and walked off to explore more of the house.

Sarah and Dave heard a noise outside and guessed it was the removals van. Dave looked at his watch, "Right on time," and went to open the front door.

Three strong young men were standing outside, while a forth, an elderly man was opening the back of the van. One of the young men spoke.

"Mr and Mrs Birch?"

"Larch," Dave quickly corrected the man.

"Oh! Ye, Larch."

Sarah went to the elderly man who was lowering the back door of the van.

"Hello Mrs Larch, fine weather it is today," the elderly man said.

"Very lucky we are," Sarah replied, "would you and the boys like a cup of tea?"

"Well, that's mighty kind of ya, but only when we've finished."

"I'll just put the kettle on so it'll be ready for you when you've finished."

It must have taken about an hour to take everything out of the van and to place everything in the house. This was the part Dave hated. The unpacking and sorting out all of the belongings.

After everyone had a good cup of refreshing tea, Dave gave

all four men twenty pounds each for being on time, and wished them a safe journey back. Dave, Sarah and Solomon were now in their new home.

Sup Sup Rose flew so fast, that on a few occasions he lost balance as he was dodging twigs, leaves and the odd insect. He always shouted sorry back to the insects in case any harm was done. Finally, he reached his destination and went straight to the elders.

"Elder Swa...Swal..." he was so out of breath he couldn't speak.

"Elder Swallowtail, I have very important ews...ews..." he paused, "news!"

Elder Perennial Swallowtail looked at Sup Sup Rose. Placing a hand on his shoulder and in a slow calming voice, he said, "Sup Sup Rose. My dear friend. Nothing can be more important than stopping yourself from choking!"

Sup Sup paused to catch his breath and apologised for the sudden outburst. Taking his time he made sure he could be understood clearly.

"I have ust...ust...just come from the ig..big tree and have seen something not right."

Two other elders came over. Anything about the big tree was always taken with keen interest.

"What have you seen?" Elder Swallowtail asked.

"From a distance, I thought I saw something that looked like a line on the tree," he noticed he was losing his speech again.

"Go on we can understand," Elder Swallowtail re-assured him.

"I flew closer and there in the re...tree, was a crack."

"A crack?" one of the elders asked.

"Yes, a rack. It wasn't old and was an ich...inch wide and a few inches long."

This alarmed the three elders, "We must inspect the tree."

Elder Swallowtail said, "And hold a meeting to tell everyone what has been discovered, but only when everyone has completed their duties to the animals."

Caitlin had arrived back, full of excitement and energy from the experience she had gained from witnessing a miracle of nature. The more experienced faeries were permitted to help out, but those who were new would have to be taught first. In the mean time, all they could do was watch and take notes as Caitlin had done. This would happen for a number of years, until they were knowledgeable enough to take on the full responsibility.

Caitlin came scurrying over a branch, when she caught a glimpse of her good and trusted friend Sup Sup Rose. She noticed that he had three elders around him and from his body language, he was very nervous. She couldn't help but be a little curious as to why, or how her friend had gotten back so quickly. She knew where he had gone to and why, but presumed she wouldn't have seen him for a few days because of the loss of his good friend.

She didn't bother going over to Sup Sup Rose and the three elders, thinking it wasn't her place. So she went back home to see what her family were doing.

A few hours had past when word got around that a meeting was being arranged, and all faeries were asked to meet up at the circle. From the gathering it looked like everyone turned up.

At the meeting there would be a very important announcement, which would affect everyone and everything in the woodland. Of course, this got everyone talking but no one could guess what. Eventually, when everything was arranged the circle was packed with every faery of all colours. There were hundreds. Some where stationed high on tree branches looking out for any unwelcome human visitors.

Boomer Safflower, a popular faery, but a little mischievous at times saw Zeal and Balamore hovering together.

"Hello," Boomer said.

"Hi, matey!" replied Balamore and Zeal.

"What's going on?" asked Boomer.

Balamore looked at Boomer and said, "Big meeting. Big news. Sup Sup has found something near, or at the big tree."

"He has!" Boomer exclaimed, "Like what!"

"That's what we're here to find out!" Zeal said.

The three of them hovered waiting for the meeting to start, when Balamore asked a question to Boomer.

"Boomer, you're late. How come?"

Boomer looked at Balamore with a face of unease. He didn't like the question, "Whenever you're late, do the elders send out a search party?"

Balamore was a bit surprised at the reaction. He never knew Boomer to have a short temper before or react in such away.

"I'm sorry, Boomer."

Boomer's face changed to a more sorrowful look, "No. I'm sorry. I was held up."

"How come?" asked Zeal.

In a low voice Boomer said, "As long as you don't tell anyone."

All three faeries moved a little closer to each other.

Boomer opened his mouth, paused and said, "I got splattered with cow manure."

His two friends started to giggle, but quickly hit each other in the ribs so they wouldn't laugh out loud. Boomer saw them holding their laughter in, then he started to smile followed by laughter as he knew it was funny. He also knew that sooner or later one of them would end up telling all their friends.

"How did that happen?" Zeal had to ask.

"I was finishing off repairing a nest for one of the wood pigeons, when I saw some moss on a field. I flew down and as I was struggling to pull it up, this big old cow just stood next to me and dropped its load."

His two friends had to let their laughter out.

Boomer continued, "Before I knew it, I was showered by the stuff. The worse thing was it was soaking wet!"

All the three of them made a noise of when someone is being sick. Then they all laughed together.

"Did you manage to finish the nest?" Balamore asked.

"No! The mother wood pigeon wouldn't let me go near the nest because of the smell."

Zeal and Balamore patted Boomer on the back and told him what a great story it was and that they were very happy to see he was all right.

After Boomer's story, the three of them and the rest of the crowd of faeries saw something happening at the meeting.

To everyone's surprise five elders of the faery order took charge of the meeting.

Elder Albizzia Silva Wood. Elder Ignis Succendo Fire. Elder Storm Marsh Fons Water. Elder Fundo Lamnia Metal, and Elder Orbis Terrarum Earth. All these Elders represented the five elements of nature. Seeing these five elders in one place at the same time sent a chilling feeling down all who gathered at the meeting.

Elder Perennial Swallowtail was asked to be with the the five elders because of his great age, experience and knowledge of many things. He was always consulted about matters of extreme importance.

The crowd that had gathered was chatting and the noise was sounding too much.

Elder Dandelion Green Leaf spoke up, "Faeries of this community, please don't be alarmed. Today is a time of great rejoicing."

Not many faeries really believed that.

"I assure you all that seeing the six elders together today, is to be viewed as merely a precaution."

"A precaution for what?" came a voice from the crowd.

Elder Swallowtail came fourth, putting a hand on Elder Dandelion's shoulder. "Allow me, my good friend." he said to Elder Dandelion, who was relieved to give up his spot to his friend.

Elder Perennial Swallowtail put his right hand in the air, and everyone stopped chatting. It was like he froze them with a spell.

"My good and kind hearted friends of the wood," his voice had an enchanting hypnotic effect upon everyone.

"Please do not be alarmed. What you see today is an event that has not happened for four hundred years. It should be viewed as a great experience to be part off." Elder Swallowtail always

73

spoke truth and no-one ever questioned his word.

"I will not deceive you today but only tell you what is."

Everyone was all ears and even the breeze in the air was still.

"Today, Sup Sup Rose, a most kind hearted and caring member of the faery community, having walked with a trusted friend to his time of passing, came across a terrible sign on the tree that keeps the Bad from escaping."

A sound of surprise was heard from a few individuals breaking the still air. It quickly quieten down and there was silence again.

"Sup Sup Rose has seen a large crack at the base of the tree. This may not seem unusual due to the course of time, but upon closer inspection by myself and the five elders, we have come to the conclusion that the spell that was placed to keep the Bad from escaping is weakening."

The voices of the crowd could not be kept down. Everyone started to talk, asking questions to one another.

"What does it mean?" a voice shouted.

"Are we safe?" another asked.

"How can this be?"

More questions were being asked.

There was panic in the air and as the noise began to get to a loud crescendo, Elder Swallowtail's colour of silver flashed brightly and brought the sound of voices to a standstill.

"DO NOT BE AFRAID!" he bellowed out to the crowd, "We are here to find a solution. We will stand together helping one another. That's what we do and that's what we do best."

In the minds of all the elders the situation looked grim. Remembering the only way the Bad was imprisoned in the first place, was because faeries and humans collaborated together and created a spell that could hold the Bad imprisoned forever.

As long as man believed in the faery tales of old, the magic keeping the Bad imprisoned would hold strong. Knowing that man had slowly left that time of magic long ago, the spell was getting weaker.

The elders had no answer and time was running out fast.

9

- FIRST SIGNS -

It had been a few weeks since Dave, Sarah and Solomon had moved into their new home They had managed to get most of the decorating done, and had arranged the furniture as they wanted. The house was looking like a proper home.

Solomon's bedroom was the first room to be decorated. Luckily, the family moved during the holidays so during that time, Solomon had tried to help out with some of the decorating.

He was given the task of choosing his own wallpaper, which he enjoyed doing. He picked an action packed wallpaper of Spiderman.

On three of his four walls, Solomon's wallpaper showed Spiderman swinging from buildings, fighting his enemies. The fourth wall had no wallpaper. He had it completely painted white like a canvas, and begged his mum to paint a picture from one of his Rupert the bear manuals. Sarah did just that, and once it was finished Solomon was very happy. Sarah was pretty pleased with herself as well.

"When I was your age, Solomon," Dave said, "I had Superman on my wall."

Sarah jumped into the father son conversation,

"Superheroes. Like father, like son."

Dave rubbed Solomon's hair, "That's my boy."

It was 7 A.M. Saturday morning. As usual, Solomon got up early. He went downstairs wearing his Rupert Bear pyjama top and bottoms, and Thomas the Tank Engine slippers.

Dave was already downstairs. He was getting ready to make a journey to Manchester to sort out some design issues. The idea of working from home was working well, and Sarah had started drawing up a plan for some painting courses.

Solomon entered the kitchen and saw his Dad, "Hi, Dad."

Dave turned round, "Morning Solomon. What would you like for breakfast?"

Solomon thought about it. He asked and was given a bowl of sugar puffs. He sat down at the kitchen table and started to spoon his mouth, which was now a docking station for the spaceship, BIG SPOON. With a crunchy sound coming from the docking station, Solomon, the Docking master announced a successful mission.

Dave heard Sarah coming downstairs, and as she entered the kitchen they both kissed each other.

"I'll be back later this afternoon," Dave said.

"Bye, Dad," Solomon said as he mumbled with a mouth full of sugar puffs.

"Bye, Solomon. Be good," Dave left the house and drove to Manchester.

After putting the kettle on, Sarah sat next to Solomon who was still crunching, "What's the plan for today, Solomon?"

Solomon swallowed his sugar puffs, "Might go to the woods."

Sarah looked at him, "Err, okay. But, if you do then I don't want you to go too far. Within calling distance."

Solomon nodded his head and kept on eating.

After breakfast Solomon went back up stairs to get ready, then came down to do a bit of drawing.

"Solomon!" Sarah shouted, "I'm going to the back garden. Do you want to go to the woods now?"

When he heard is Mum's voice he jumped off the suite,

making sure that Rupert the bear was in his hand. He ran to his mother, who was now walking into the garden with a sketch pad and an assortment of pencils.

The sun was shining and the whole sky was blue. There wasn't a cloud in sight. The two of them walked together outside and were greeted with a rainbow of colours. Blues, pinks, violets, indigo's, reds and whites, where all dazzling to their eyes, "Gosh, isn't it beautiful, Solomon?" Sarah asked.

"Fantastic," he answered.

Sarah had seen an opportunity to do a bit of sketching of some flowers she had seen in the back garden. The flowers in the garden were all in full bloom, and the lawn was a vibrant colour of green.

Surrounding the garden was another dry stone wall, just like at the front of the house. The wall was covered with an array of wild flowers, herbs and moss. The dry stone wall looked old, with odd shaped blocks of stone placed on top of each other, resembling a squiggly line. The stone was sturdy, with the odd weed peeping through the aged old cracks. Parts of the wall was covered with moss. Beautiful in colour, it was soft to the touch just like velvet. It was a perfect scene for Sarah to sketch.

At the back of the garden there were a few wooden steps that had been carefully built into the stone wall. Solomon saw the steps, let go of his mother's hand and said, "I'm off."

Sarah, feeling her son's excitement said, "Don't go off too far. When I call you, you be straight back."

Solomon had already reached the step when he shouted back, "WILL DO," then he was up and over and into the woods that was at the back of the garden wall. As soon as he had entered the wood, Solomon had entered a whole new world.

His imagination started to race ahead. In his mind, he was in a place where only the bravest of the brave would survive. With his trusted side companion, Rupert, the two of them ventured to do battle with imaginary beasts, and help out the enchanting little people who lived in the trees. Unbeknownst to Solomon, the wood did hold the little people that are found in books as well as ghosts, ghouls and the oakmen who went around the woods to nurture and protect the trees and animals.

He went further in to the wood. He was looking at the tall, elegant, old trees that surrounded him. Compared to them he was just a midget, and felt like one of the little people he had read about in one of his many faery tale books. Solomon suddenly stopped walking.

Just ahead of him he saw a hedgehog, wobbling through the undergrowth looking for food. Then he saw a group of rabbits jumping and running about. He was mesmerised by the sight. Never in his life had he seen such wonders, except on TV. Seeing it for real was a dream come true.

He crouched down slowly and silently and kept on looking. Minutes felt like hours while he was watching the rabbits jump. After a few moments he got up. Knees soiled from crouching on the woodland floor. He started to walk through the wood again, venturing further in and away from home.

He had walked some considerable distance, when he noticed that he couldn't see the house from where he was. A slight fear started to take hold of him and he wondered what to do. He turned in all directions, but couldn't understand where the path that he had just travelled had gone. With Rupert being held close to his chest, he walked in the direction he thought he had come from.

After a short while, he knew that he didn't recognise any of the trees that he had passed. He couldn't find the place that he saw the rabbits at or where the hedgehog was. He started to feel a little scared and started to make a slight weeping sound. With Rupert held close he didn't know what to do, and when he was just about to let out a loud wail of a cry, something caught his eye.

A small light was moving fast towards him. Zigzagging around trees and up over branches. A voice could be heard saying, "Don't cry little one, you are safe."

Solomon forgot about crying and was transfixed upon the light that was getting closer and closer, until it was floating in mid air right at the tip of his nose.

Solomon looked closely and saw a young girl wearing a very small dress that looked like it was made of gold.

"A faery!" Solomon exclaimed.

The faery just giggled and kissed his nose.

"Now, don't be scared. I'm here to help you get home," the voice of the faery said.

Solomon's face lit up when he heard the word home.

He plucked up the courage and said, "Hello. I'm Solomon."

The faery whizzed around Solomon's head until she was back in front of his face.

"Nice to meet you, Solomon. I'm Caitlin. Caitlin Lavender."

Solomon didn't know what else to say, but just kept on looking.

"And who is that you are holding?" Caitlin asked, looking at the toy bear Solomon was holding.

Solomon looked at it and said, "This is my best friend, Rupert."

Caitlin smiled and thought it was so sweet and very typical and innocent of a child.

Caitlin floated down to Solomon's free hand, lifted his whole hand up, took hold of one of his little fingers and said, "I think it's time you were going home."

Solomon felt a slight tug and he started to walk forward.

During the time Caitlin was showing Solomon the way home, she told him about the many wonderful things in the wood. About how the faeries help the animals, trees and flowers. How if an animal is sick, the faeries will come to its aid and nurture it back to health. After that, Solomon said that he wanted to be an animal doctor and Caitlin just laughed. She loved to hear the voices of children speak.

He was also told about the great battle where mankind, myths, legends and folklore teamed up to fight a great and terrifying evil monster. That they defeated it and imprisoned it for all eternity. Solomon couldn't believe such a battle could have happened and was so excited hearing about it. The more he got excited the more Caitlin's colour shone brighter. Even when the sun was shining her colour of gold was still clearly visible.

Just as Caitlin was coming to the end of a story she was telling Solomon, the two of them saw the garden wall that led onto the garden of Solomon's house.

"Here we are Solomon. Safe and sound," Caitlin said.

Solomon looked at her, "Would you like to come in. My mum would like to thank you for bringing me home."

Caitlin's face beamed with a smile. She fluttered to his forehead and kissed it ever so gently.

"I'm afraid I cannot do that Solomon. I must be getting home myself. Maybe we will see each other again."

Solomon's face flushed with excitement.

"Goodbye, Solomon," Caitlin said and before Solomon could say thank you, she was gone as if she was never there.

Solomon ran up and over the garden wall towards his mother. Sarah was finishing off a sketch and was about to call Solomon, when she saw him running down the garden path. He came to a skidding halt and told her at a 100 words a minute, his little adventure with a faery called Caitlin.

After about five minutes of listening to the story, and four times telling Solomon to slow down, she grabbed him in her arms and said, "How about a nice big sandwich and a glass of milk?"

Solomon held up his arms in the air and shouted, "YE!"

The two of them went inside the house and from a distance on a tree branch, Caitlin watched feeling happy that Solomon was safe.

"Keep telling her, Solomon," Caitlin whispered to herself, "she'll never believe you."

Deep down she did wish that his mother would believe him. She wished that everyone would believe, like the time when humans and faeries co-existed together. When Caitlin saw the back door of the house close, she jumped of the tree and flew back home to her own family, having a feeling that she may soon meet Solomon again.

As Caitlin flew away, she did not notice another pair of eyes that had been watching her and the boy walking together. These eyes did not show love or goodness in them. They had a tinge of corruption and the animal that had these eyes had a plan. A wicked plan that would use Caitlin, the boy and the rest of the faery nation.

80

Within a flash the creature was gone. All that was left, were the songs of birds singing and a slight rustling of leaves as they were gently being caressed by a breeze.

For now, the wood was a very calm and peaceful place.

10

- STORIES -

Dave arrived back home around twelve thirty in the afternoon.

"Dad! Dad!" Solomon was jumping up and down with excitement.

Dave knelt down and kissed his son on the cheek, "What is it tiger?"

Before Dave could get back up on his feet, Solomon had his hand and was trying to drag him to the back garden.

Helping her husband up, Sarah said to him, "Has he got a tale to tell you."

Dave allowed himself to be dragged to the back garden and to the back wall, where Solomon started to tell his father of the wonderful meeting he had with a faery called Caitlin. How the faeries are worried about a thing called the Bad. Dave was smiling and loving every minute of the story, especially the part when Caitlin, who was so tiny picked up Solomon's hand and guided him through the wood. Eventually, Solomon finished the story.

Dave looked at his son, "Solomon, that's an amazing story. You really should write that down."

At last Solomon's enthusiasm wore off, because his stomach started to rumble. The three of them went back into the house for something to eat. After some big sandwiches that Sarah made, they all decided to go out for a walk around the village of Birchover.

Dave loved the country air and Sarah was happy also. Solomon was extremely excited. He had never felt like this in the city and it made his mum and dad feel that they had made the right decision to move. The family spent a few hours in the village, looking at the sights and listening to the sounds of the village.

The scenery was breathtaking, and Sarah jotted down in a notebook she had brought with her, what future sketches and paintings she would start with. It was turning out to be a great weekend, and one that they hadn't had to do any decorating or moving of furniture. Dave bought everyone an ice cream and they walked over to a bench that was in the shade of a tree.

"Mum," Solomon said.

"*Slurp, slurp*" was the only sound his mum could make, not able to talk because of the delicious ice cream.

"Can you do some drawings for me?"

"What would you like me to draw?"

"Faeries!"

Dave smiled and looked at Sarah, "Why do you want me to draw faeries?" Sarah asked.

"Because I want to give Caitlin a drawing. To say thanks."

Sarah placed her hand on his head and said, "I think it would be better if the drawing came from you."

Solomon looked puzzled, "Why?" he asked.

"Because when Caitlin sees that it's from your own hands, the thanks you are saying will mean so much more."

Solomon sat there and thought about it for a while, at the same time licking the ice cream that had dribbled down his hands, "Okay," he said, "I'll do it," he then thrust his already ice cream covered lips into the cone and sucked hard.

They all got back home later that day after having their fill of ice cream. Sarah had made lots of notes of what places would be nice to paint and sketch, while Dave was just taking it easy and forgetting everything that was about work.

The three of them entered the house and Solomon shot upstairs.

"Solomon, what are you doing?" Sarah asked.

"I'm going to do a drawing for Caitlin," Solomon bellowed from the top of the stairs.

"There's nothing wrong with a pretend friend," Dave said to Sarah. He then grabbed and tickled her.

Sarah exploded with laughter. Dave definitely knew where her sensitive spots were.

Just as they had both rolled over the suite and onto the floor, the door bell rang. Dave now with his hair brushed forward and over his eyes jumped up wondering who it could be. Sarah got up and straightened her clothes. Dave brushed his hair back with his hands. He walked over to the front door and opened it.

An elderly woman stood there in the door way looking at Dave. She saw that Dave still had half his shirt hanging out of his pants.

"Oh! Er, hello. How can I help you?" Dave asked the elderly lady.

"Oops! I'm so sorry to disturb you. I wonder if you might have anything to give away," the lady asked.

Dave looked a little confused, "Excuse me!"

"Oh! I'm sorry. Did you not receive this?"

The elderly lady held up a small plastic package with the word, 'DONATIONS' in big red letters, "I'm collecting for UNICEF."

Dave now looked like he understood, "I'm terribly sorry. We've just moved in and I don't recall getting anything like that."

The woman smiled, "May I leave this with you and come back at a later time?"

Sarah walked forward and joined in the conversation, "Hello, we have some old stuff upstairs that you can have."

The elderly lady smiled greatly, "That's so kind of you."

84

Without hesitation, Sarah invited the lady in to the house and the elderly lady stepped in. She went over and stood by the TV. Without a minute gone by, Solomon came flying in to the living room where the three of them were standing.

"Hello my dear," the elderly lady spoke slow and elegantly.

Solomon stood on his toes and started to rock to and fro, wondering what to do. Without being asked he walked straight up to the lady.

To Dave and Sarah's surprise, Solomon held out his hand. The elderly lady placed her gloved hand into his and they both shook.

"What a gentleman you are Solomon."

Sarah moved forward slightly and said, "How did you know his name?"

The elderly lady let go of Solomon's hand and looked at both Dave and Sarah, "Why, news travels fast in a village such as Birchover."

Dave and Sarah's face looked a little relieved, if not still a little confused.

"I guess we'll still have to get use to that," Sarah said.

The elderly woman chuckled, "Oh, where are my manners. I am Winnie. Winnie Tucker."

Dave and Sarah shook her hand and Dave asked, "Are you a local?"

Winnie gave out a smile that only pleasant little old ladies could give.

"I am. In fact, I am your neighbour."

Sarah and Dave felt at ease now and invited Winnie to sit down, which she graciously did.

Winnie saw a picture that Solomon had drawn and asked about it.

"Solomon, may I call you Solomon?" Solomon nodded with great enthusiasm, "May I look at your picture?"

Solomon gladly showed Winnie his picture and when she saw it, she gave Solomon great praises.

"My, my, you are a true artist. This is wonderful."

Solomon's face glowed from the praise. He couldn't keep

his excitement in as he was hopping on both feet.

"Now, let me see." Winnie was looking at the picture carefully. She scrutinised the colours and the figures that Solomon had drawn.

"Mmm," she quietly said. Winnie started to follow an invisible line with her finger. Her finger stopped when it came to a figure coloured in a bright yellow.

"Solomon, is this Caitlin?"

Dave and Sarah's mouths dropped to the floor and Solomon got even more excited, knowing that there was someone else who knew Caitlin.

Solomon screamed, "YES!"

Winnie laughed and gave Solomon a big hug, "You are a very lucky boy. Treasure the moment you met her. Never forget it."

After giving Winnie a cup of tea, Sarah said to her, "You really don't have to encourage him."

"Encourage!" Winnie exclaimed, "I'm not encouraging him. I'm helping him understand what he saw was true. That's the problem with the world today. When we grow up we forget what we knew as little children. The innocent stories that we were told are not just stories, but are true."

Everything Winnie was saying she could see was going over Sarah and Dave's heads. And they were probably thinking she was some batty old lady. She quickly drank her tea.

"I must be leaving now," she said, "I can see in your eyes that you think I am some crazy fuddy duddy old granny."

"No, no, it isn't like that," Sarah quickly said, "It's just that fantasies like that are just stories. Sooner or later, Solomon will have to realise its just all make believe." Sarah was feeling a little uncomfortable now.

Winnie looked at both Sarah and Dave with eyes that felt sorry for both of them.

"My dear, in this world there is more than just what we see and take for granted. There is a world that children readily accept and we forget."

Winnie knew it would take more than words to convince Sarah and Dave. She stood up and told the two of them that she must leave.

Winnie got to the front door holding a bag of clothes that Sarah had given to her. Dave opened the front door. As Winnie was stepping outside, she turned to Solomon who was standing next to his mother and said to him.

"Solomon, never forget what you saw today. You must believe and if you do, the faeries will be your friends for life."

Sarah smiled thinking it was just helping Solomon adjust to the new surroundings.

After saying goodbye Winnie walked away. The door closed and as Winnie was walking down the street she said to herself, "Solomon, you must keep believing."

For the rest of the day Solomon, Dave and Sarah went to the back garden and enjoyed the bright sunshine and the fresh air.

- PROMISES -

A flutter of wings was buzzing around the old ancient oak tree that held the Bad imprisoned. As the flutter of wings hovered over the crack that had formed in the tree, a voice spoke out.

"Soon Master, you will be set free. This time you will rule this world."

A groaning noise came from beneath the tree as if agreeing, and then the buzzing sound of the wings flew away leaving a silence in the air.

- SURPRISING NEWS -

It was late afternoon and Solomon was sitting down on the suite watching TV, when his mother walked into the room holding two glasses of cool fresh milk.

"Here you are tiger," she said holding out a glass for him.

Solomon took the glass, "Thanks Mum," and happily gulped the contents of the glass down, before his mother had taken her first sip.

Looking at her son, she asked, "What are you watching, Solomon?"

"The news," Solomon answered.

"The news!" she exclaimed.

"Sure. It's exciting."

Solomon turned up the volume and Sarah wondered what could possibly be exciting. The newsreader's voice was heard through the speakers of the TV.

"During the past week, people have been reporting unexplained phenomena that have started to appear up and down the country. Our local reporter Desmond Page, is at the scene of a reported sighting."

The news switched to the reporter standing in a field with a group of people standing behind him.

"People have claimed to witness dragons flying in the sky. Pigmies, dwarfs and big ugly trolls. The scientific community have issued an explanation stating, these apparent sightings can be explained by the sudden heat wave of the British Summer."

Solomon's face reflected excitement when he heard the names of mythical beasts.

"The heat reflecting of the roads creates an illusion, so the general public could be duped in to believing they are seeing fictitious characters from fantasy novels."

Sarah giggled a little and Solomon nudged her in the ribs. They both continued to watch until the report had finished. Solomon turned the TV off and stood up.

"And where do you think you are going?" Sarah asked.

"Out to the garden. To look for more faeries and trolls," answered Solomon.

Sarah had to smile at his innocence.

Solomon just turned and ran to the garden. Once he got there, the sun was breaking through the clouds not allowing them to have their way.

The rays of sunshine seemed to turn up the colour of green in the grass. Bees buzzed about checking every flower they could find, searching for nectar. Butterflies looked like they were dancing as they fluttered about the garden. He loved the place around him.

He started to check the flowers the soil and the grass, but couldn't find what he wanted to see. He then raised his head and looked at the wood.

It stood as it had always stood tall, old, yet a feeling of foreboding came from the place that not long ago showed him the good spirit of the wood. Caitlin the faery.

His curiosity was getting the better of him and was egging him to go back into the wood. As he stepped closer to the garden wall that touched the edge of the wood, Solomon heard his mother's voice shouting him to come in for something to eat. Dave came running out of the house and scooped Solomon up into his arms.

"My goodness Solomon you are getting heavy."

Solomon screamed with pleasure and Dave took him back into the house.

From the edge of the wood a set of golden coloured wings hovered above the ground. Caitlin watched the two of them having fun.

"Solomon. You and Winnie must help your parents believe," she then flew away deep into the woods.

For the next few days, the great British weather turned and an ocean of rain fell upon the village. It wasn't all bad. The countryside got a good watering after the scorching sun. The rain cooled the area down. Even with the rain pouring you could still find the ice cream van driving around, and local ramblers trekking through the woods and over fields.

To everyone in the village this was typical of the weather for this time of year, but to the creatures of the wood, it meant more.

With sightings being reported by people something magical was going to happen, but also something was coming that nobody wanted.

It wasn't going to be good for anyone.

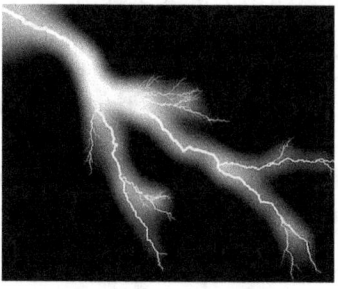

13

- DESPERATE TIMES -

During the course of a debate, those that attended the faery meeting came to a decision that a careful watch was needed over the tree. With continuing arguments over the future of the wood and maybe the world, it had become a precarious time for all that lived in the wood. With word from the elders, Zeal and Balamore had organised groups to watch over the tree day and night.

Everyone who participated believed it to be important and necessary. In everyone's eyes, it would take as long as it needed to take until the right answer came along.

Everyone was feeling a little nervous about the whole affair, but it had to be done. The most worried faery was Elder Perennial Swallowtail. He was certain the Bad would escape very soon.

Over the course of a month, Sarah with the help of Dave and Solomon, had written and designed a painting course for artists, or those who just wanted to somehow express their artistic ideas on canvas. With the local village being used as subject matter, Sarah believed that she had created what people wanted. Nothing too difficult or expensive, but challenging enough to get the painter enthused about the subject.

After Sarah was satisfied with the program, Dave designed some advertising and printed up some flyers, while Solomon drew up his own subjects that he thought would be great to paint. Dragons, trolls and of course faeries. Funnily enough, Solomon had kept paper clippings from newspapers. These paper clippings were about the mysterious sightings, the legendary creatures that people have reported seeing. Hoping deep down in his heart he wished that he would be one of those people who would see a creature.

One night during the week Solomon was trying to get to sleep. Holding on to Rupert the bear tightly, he watched and listened to the rain outside. It was a heavy storm. Lightning and heavy rain fell. Raindrops hit the window hard, sounding like a bucket full of nails being thrown onto a tin roof. Solomon had visions of it trying to break the glass so it could swallow him up. He held onto Rupert even tighter.

A bright flash of light and a roar of thunder erupted, electrifying the black rain clouds, illuminating the sky and showing their twisted distorted faces to whom was watching.

Solomon pulled up his bed quilt closer to his face and said to Rupert, "It's okay. I'll protect you," another bolt of lightning flashed and Solomon squeezed Rupert even more until the little bear looked anorexic.

Back in the wood the faeries looking after the tree were sheltering from the ravaging thunderstorm. A young faery called Brandy Bluebell, had to dart to one side before a large branch came crashing down.

Out of nowhere silver white light could be seen coming towards them. It was Elder Swallowtail. At lightning speed he headed towards those who were sheltering. He stopped and hovered above the crack in the tree. As the others looked they noticed that the raindrops that were showering the wood were not hitting him, the rain just veered around him.

Elder Swallowtail looked at Brandy Bluebell and the other faeries, "I'll teach you this trick another day," and winked at them. He then fluttered down to the crack and examined it closely.

"Oh dear!" he quietly said, "this is very grim."

As he spoke, a lightning bolt struck the crack exploding the wood of the tree upon impact, and at the same time sending Elder Swallowtail hurtling away.

Smoke filled the air making it difficult to see. After a little while as the falling rain cleared the smoke away, everyone who was there saw the damage caused by the lightning strike.

Where there used to be a small crack in the tree there was now a large hole.

Everyone around looked in disbelief, unprepared by the sudden catastrophe that had befallen them. Some of the faeries were flying round and round confused and dazed. The only one who was calm and composed was Elder Swallowtail. The lightning and falling rain helped create a more confusing situation.

Elder Swallowtail moved closer to the large hole. After a brief moment he turned around and saw many other elders coming forward. It was time for action.

He flew towards them with a hand in the air to reassure everyone. For the time being everything was fine. Now he addressed the other elders.

"Elders, we must quickly form a spell and fill in the hole before any other damage happens."

The other elders quickly agreed and gathered as many adult faeries as possible.

Everyone gathered and surrounded the tree like a circle of light. Dozens of faeries gathered around the tree linking arm to arm, until it looked like an unbreakable ring of rainbow colours.

The elders started to chant a song in a language that had not been heard in a millennia, while the other faeries held each other tight and waited.

As the sound of the song rang through the forest, the glow of colour glowed brighter and brighter, until at a certain moment the mixture of colours surrounded the whole tree like a veil of soft silk. From root to tip of every branch nothing was left uncovered.

This went on until Elder Perennial Swallowtail slowly moved away from the tree, still attached to the circle by a line of throbbing gold, red and purple light emitting from his body.

When he was a few feet from the tree the other elders did the same creating a star like shape, all connected by a line of light throbbing with vibrant colours. When Elder Swallowtail was ready he gave a sign.

His whole body of light changed to green, which was immediately copied by the other elders. The light of all faeries faded leaving the tree covered by the veil of green light, which then changed to white.

All moved away looking starry eyed at the tree. After Elder Swallowtail and the other elders checked the tree, everyone moved deeper into the wood until they gathered together as a large group. Elder Swallowtail took charge and quickly calmed everyone's fears.

"Please. Please, everyone, I will not hide the truth from you as that is not my nature. Tonight has been a frightening time and one that needs careful consideration."

Everyone mumbled. Some confused. Some shaking from fear but all of them wanted to know what was to be done.

Elder Dandelion Green Leaf came forward and said, "My dear brothers, sisters, family and friends. The unthinkable has happened. Tonight the great storm that we have all been fearing has come. And it has broken the spell that was cast a thousand years ago. The age of mystical age is coming to an end unless we can find a lasting solution. The veil of light we have put on the tree will not last long."

A noise of worry came from the crowd.

"How long?" someone shouted.

With a look of worry on Elder Dandelion's face he said, "A week. Maybe less. Depends on the damage and how strong the thing that lives below the tree is."

Everyone was feeling restless. Just then, one faery flew through the crowd and addressed everyone. It was Caitlin.

"Everyone. Listen to what the elders have to say," she

needed to say something to the crowd.

"We must believe in them. Ask yourself, have they ever let you down, misled you, or ever given you thoughts of distrust? NEVER! We all knew this time was going to come. We must accept it now or forever lose the battle before we have fought. Let us not give up before we have even started. There is always hope, even in times of desperation."

An elder flew over to Caitlin and placed his hand on her shoulder. All that were present knew she was right and that there was hope, but where? They had to find it.

Far in the distance outside of the wood, unbeknownst to the creatures some humans had seen the lightning strike and the sudden glowing light coming from the tree.

Winnie Tucker leapt out of bed, being awakened by the terrific storm that was erupting outside her window. She quickly put on her dressing gown, walked to her bedroom window and opened the curtains. A sudden flash of streaking white light erupted in front of her and then another. At the same time, a loud cracking sound then bellowing thunder filled the sky. So loud was the thunder that it seemed that the whole night sky had split in two.

Winnie looked on and stared at the woodland at the bottom of her garden. She was peering at only one thing, the area that held the great tree. Deep down she felt worried, not for herself but for those that were guarding the tree. Another bolt shot from the sky, only this time it wasn't just the sky that lit up, it was the place that Winnie was looking at.

Winnie saw the lightning bolt strike at the very heart of the wood and after a few seconds, a yellow flash of light lit the sky.

"OH! NO!" Winnie cried out.

Winnie knew what had just happened. She knew that the tree in the wood that was keeping the Bad from escaping, had been struck. Her heart fell to the ground but there was nothing she could do right now. While the rain was pouring and the lightning was flashing, it was simply too dangerous to go out. Her heart was feeling for the little creatures of the wood and knew she had to do something.

She rushed downstairs and opened the back door to the

garden. Wind and rain lashed out at her telling her to stay back. With a long rain coat as protection she fought her way to her wooden shed. As she got to the garden shed door, she unlatched it and fell in just keeping her balance.

"There we are," she whispered.

Winnie looked around the shed and saw what she was looking for. With the lightning flashing across the sky she didn't need a torch to find what she wanted. She picked up a small three step ladder, and from a wooden shelf attached to the shed's wall a box of matches.

She opened up the ladders and moved them to one end of the shed. Carefully she stepped on to the ladder. Striking a match the glow of the flame gave light to the building, illuminating everything inside.

In front of her were two oil lamps hanging from the ceiling. Winnie immediately lit the two lamps and as soon as the match made contact with the wick, the lamps lit into life. Winnie did the same to another two lamps at the other end of the shed. Four oil lamps were now burning brightly. The light source was beaming through the plain glass windows of the shed.

She stepped down and looked at the burning lamps.

"As promised, a light for all those lost little creatures," she said, "come, come don't be afraid."

As if by magic a few very small lights came flying into the shed, via a few well made holes. The lights buzzed around Winnie's head and rested on her shoulder.

"Oh, my little friends. I'm so happy I wasn't too late," she excitedly exclaimed, "are there any more coming?"

A few of the lights glowed intensely, indicating a positive yes. Just then a flapping nose came from below Winnie's feet and she saw three badgers coming into the shed, through a well used cat flap that had been made in the door. Following the badgers were a couple of foxes.

Seeing these creatures made Winnie more relaxed. She bent down with a cloth in her hands and started to gently rub the water from the backs of the badgers and foxes. After she had wiped the animals dry, she told them to wait while she went out to get something.

Just a few moments had passed when Winnie arrived back with a box full of bread, dog food, a few bottles of milk and some fruit. She wasn't going to let the poor animals starve. She gently placed everything down on to the floor. The badgers and foxes just waited for the portions, not even rushing forward to grab the food.

There were now more faeries in the shed than before and they were also very grateful for the food. Showing their gratitude, they caressed Winnie's face and helped dry her wet hair. After a while, she sat down on the floor watching the creatures eat and drink. Occasionally, she would talk to the faeries.

After the creatures had their full they walked over to Winnie. Badgers, foxes and a few of the very young faeries nestled into her, sharing their body heat with Winnie. With a quick wave of a hand from a faery, the lights from the oil burners dimmed and all who were in the shed fell asleep. The only sound that could be heard, was the splatter of rain hitting the windows of the shed. The lightning had stopped and the wind had calmed down.

The other people who saw the lightning strike were Solomon, who was getting a little scared and his father, Dave who was with him.

They both saw the massive explosion erupting from the wood and after a few minutes, the glow of light.

"Can we go and see Dad? Can we?" Solomon asked impatiently.

"In the morning, Solomon," Dave said, "we'll go and check it out in the morning."

That got Solomon excited but didn't calm him down. Dave helped Solomon into bed, pulled up the bed quilt over him and kissed him goodnight.

He looked at his son and said, "First thing in the morning, Solomon," that brought a big smile on Solomon's face.

Within minutes he was fast a sleep dreaming of adventures in the wood.

14

- SECRETS REVEALED -

The next morning, Winnie woke up with a bright beam of sun dancing over her face. She looked around and all the creatures were gone. She smiled happily and was proud that she was of some help.

She picked up the empty bottles of milk and cans of food and headed back to the house. As she was walking through her garden, she looked back in the direction of the wood and said to herself, "I must see how the tree is."

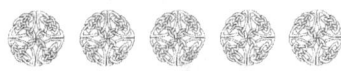

As promised, first thing in the morning right after breakfast Dave took Solomon to the wood, but Sarah didn't let them go unprepared. She had made a box full of sandwiches for their journey. As soon as Dave was given them he placed the box in a small ruck sack and off they went.

The ground was muddy and Solomon loved it. Both of them were wearing Wellington boots. Dave's were green and well used, and Solomon's were red with Rupert the bear on the sides.

The two of them walked across the garden over the wall

and stepped into the wood. Solomon, at the first sign of a muddy puddle couldn't resist and jumped as high as he could, landing with both feet firmly into the middle of the puddle, spraying the muddy water everywhere. He was having a fun time and so was Dave. Just to watch Solomon behave like this was a thrill, compared to seeing Solomon cough and splutter when they lived in the city. Even Dave joined in with jumping into the puddles.

They both held hands walking through the wood, and Solomon started to pull his father deeper into the woodland. Dave wondered how his son knew where to go. Occasionally, he would let Solomon run ahead knowing he wanted to be the guide and explorer. But he made sure he had a close eye on his son.

They continued walking and jumping, until Solomon shouted at his Dad, "There! There!"

Dave ran towards Solomon and grabbed his hand. He asked him what he could see.

Solomon pointed and as Dave looked, he thought he could see a glimmer of light.

As they continued to walk closer and closer to the light, the two of them stood in awe looking at the white pulsating light that covered the tree. The whole tree was brilliant white, but not too bright that it would blind you.

Solomon started to pull his dad closer to the tree.

"Solomon no! We don't know what's going on. What has happened," Dave said, feeling a little nervous if not curious.

"It's okay, Dad. Everything is safe. The faeries did this," Solomon said, with a rising confidence in his voice.

Dave still couldn't believe it. "Faeries!" he said.

Then out of the blue a voice came from the side, "Yes! Faeries."

Dave and Solomon turned round and saw Winnie Tucker standing there. She was smiling from ear to ear.

She was wearing long pink pants, the bottom part of the legs tucked into her red Doc Martin boots. Her thick long overcoat, was made up from different coloured squares all carefully sewn together. She wore a long multi-coloured scarf wrapped around her neck. On top of her head was a blue woolly hat, with the word

'Rupert' embroidered on it.

She stepped forward taking her hat off, and as she approached Solomon she knelt down and gently placed it on top of his head.

Dave looked at Winnie as she stood up and asked her, "Faeries? What do you mean?"

Winnie looked at him, knowing full well that it was always the adults that found it the hardest to believe.

"Like I said, faeries. They are here. All around us. Solomon has seen them, haven't you Solomon?" Winnie asked as she looked at him.

Solomon nodded excitedly, hoping to see a faery again. Winnie looked into Dave's eyes knowing what was coming next.

"Are you seriously saying that faeries are real? That they live here in the wood?" Dave gestured with his arms in disbelief.

"Let me ask you a question," Winnie said, "When you were a child did you not believe in the tooth faery, in dragons, trolls and mythical creatures of the wood?"

Dave listened and stuttered his answer, "Su...Sure. Every kid did."

"So what has changed?"

Dave smiled thinking he knew the answer.

"We grow up. We find out that they're just stories to entertain us as kids. Nothing like that could ever be true."

Just then a black shadow flew over head making a loud whooshing sound.

"What was that?" Dave quickly asked.

Winnie looked up into the sky and said, "The mythical creatures you don't believe."

She again looked at Dave, "See the tree. Why do you think it's glowing?"

Dave looked at it closely until he felt himself feeling very calm and relaxed.

He closed his eyes and without moving could sense he was falling backwards. He didn't open his eyes, he didn't want to. He just let himself fall. The feeling was like a slow journey across peaceful water. An untouched lake with only himself crossing it.

He could feel a warm feeling on the back of his neck like a beautiful summer day, with the sun just letting out enough heat that it was pleasant and perfect. He still had his eyes closed and had no feelings to open them. He concentrated on the noises he could hear.

The noise came from cool air brushing across his face. It was strange. Just after he felt the cool air it changed to warm air.

He could now hear the noise of clashing steel then an explosion. Men shouting could be heard. Loud screeching sounds of what he thought were arrows flying, passing his ears. Still, he kept his eyes shut but could see everything clearly with his mind's eye.

Explosions erupted over his head, which made him jump up quickly. With a sudden shock, Dave felt himself hit something soft and soggy. He opened his eyes and saw himself flat faced in the mud at the feet of his son.

Solomon was giggling for fun, while his dad lifted himself up off the ground slightly bewildered and dirty.

Looking at Winnie, Dave asked, "Wh...What just happened?"

"A dream? A nightmare? Images from the past? What you saw could be any of them or all." Winnie answered.

Dave looked more and more confused. He grabbed Solomon's hand and tugged him to tell him that they were both leaving.

"Dad." Solomon moaned, "What about the tree?"

Dave looked at it. No trees ever shone like this one did. Dave had no answers but he felt that both of them should stay and find out.

Looking at Winnie he said, "Okay. I'm all ears. What is going on? Why is this tree glowing?"

Sighing with relief, Winnie pointed at an old broken up tree that was jutting out of the ground. She asked the two of them to sit down on the stump. All three of them sat down and Winnie started to tell them what she knew.

"I've lived around these woods for an awfully long time, and I've been entrusted with secrets that would surprise the most open minded of folk." Winnie wriggled on the tree stump to get comfortable, then continued.

"Ever since I was a little girl, I was first introduced to the faeries of these woods by my mother. Who was introduced to them by her mother, and so on." She paused to take a breath, "There are a few others in the village who know of the secrets of the wood, but not many."

Winnie looked at Solomon and said, "Solomon is very privileged to know about them so quickly."

She then asked him, "Caitlin, she was the one wasn't she?"

Solomon nodded and said, "Yes. Yes she was."

Without hesitation, she said to the two of them, "You must see more of them."

Dave couldn't quite understand what was happening, but went along with it. However, Solomon on the other hand just couldn't keep his excitement in.

"Follow me," Winnie said, and she led them away from the glowing tree to a place that was circular and wide.

The three of them stopped walking. Winnie knelt down and rested on her knees. She then gently blew into the air. For a short while nothing happened until Solomon saw it coming fast from among the trees. He tugged his father's coat sleeve and pointed in the direction of the moving object.

Four large badgers came rushing through the trees and straight towards Winnie. She looked at Solomon and Dave and asked them to kneel down. They both did, and when the badgers came close enough, Winnie took Solomon's hand and gently placed it on the back of one of the badgers. As soon as his fingers caressed the soft thick fur of the nearest badger, half a dozen bright lights shot from the badger's coat and flew around Solomon and Dave's head

"I...I...I don't believe it." was all Dave could say, seeing the tiniest most beautiful and purest of faces floating just a few inches away from his nose.

Solomon was wide eyed and beaming with a smile. Winnie looked around to see how many there were. As she was counting, more of the little dandy creatures floated, whizzed and zigzagged about. Then there was one that caught her eye. Winnie asked

Solomon to look and when he did, he instantly recognised the faery.

"Caitlin!" he screamed out in delight.

That got Dave's attention. When he saw her he couldn't believe how beautiful she was. Gentle in features and heart warming in colour, her golden light lit the faces of both Dave and Solomon.

Caitlin stroked Solomon's nose, which tickled him into a little giggle. She fluttered to Dave. Looking at him, she bowed and said in her gentle and enchanting voice, "Welcome to the circle of magic."

More lights appeared, and at one point it looked like Winnie, Dave and Solomon were surrounded by hundreds of bright, glistening lights of different colours. Dave just knelt there stunned at what he was seeing.

All the stories that he had been told and had dismissed when he grew up, were now real. All true. Not one a lie or made up story. He was experiencing what he only had imagined when he was a young boy.

To Dave everything seemed perfect like living the most wonderful dream. This time he wasn't going to wake up and find out it was a dream, he was living the dream for real.

A few very curious faeries who were plump in appearance, flew straight towards Dave and darted through his hair. This sent a strange tingling sensation down Dave's neck. A lovely feeling of pleasure and fun. He grinned from ear to ear like a Cheshire cat and felt like he was 10 years old again.

He looked down at Solomon and said, "How the heck are we going to explain this to your mother? I'll never know."

Solomon kept on giggling and loving every moment.

Both of them were loving the attention from their new found friends. Solomon knew all along he was right and was happy that his father knew as well. Winnie was also enjoying the moment. She loved spending time in the wood and helping out the animals the best she could.

From a distance watching what was going on, an elder of the faeries approached. Gracefully moving forward in the air.

104

As he came closer, the other faeries parted to let him through. He stopped a few inches from Dave's face and with a smile, his silver colour glowed.

He introduced himself to Dave.

"I am Elder Perennial Swallowtail," Dave looked on in awe, "I am one of the elders that live in this wood."

Just then other elders appeared. All of them fluttered and floated around Dave and Solomon.

Dave smiled with excitement.

"Hello everyone," was the only thing he could think of still shocked at what was happening.

The other faeries were hanging around Winnie, who was giving out bread crumbs from her coat pocket to each one of them.

As soon as all the elders had introduced themselves, Zeal White Oak and Balamore Skullcap rushed forward and grabbed Dave's thumb, lifting it up and shaking it. Dave nearly jumped back in surprise by the sheer strength of Zeal and Balamore.

"Hey! How are you? Great to see you. Are you going to help us?" both Zeal and Balamore saying the same words at the same time, trying to out word each other.

"Help?" Dave said, "Help you with what?"

Zeal and Balamore gently let go of his thumb and fluttered over to their friend Caitlin. Elder Dandelion Green Leaf spoke.

"A terrible thing has befallen this wood and the community of animals that dwell here."

Dave listened hard, while Solomon was playing with Caitlin, Zeal and Balamore.

"As you have probably seen, there is a great tree that does not look like a tree any more."

Dave thought about it and replied, "Oh, the white glowing tree."

Elder Dandelion Green Leaf looked at Dave with caring eyes and said, "Yes, the white tree," he moved closer and continued.

"It is the oldest tree in the wood and a protector of everything alive including your world." Elder Green Leaf's face grew slightly serious, not towards Dave but towards the thought of what may happen in the future.

"May I ask, what do you mean?" Dave asked.

Elder Dandelion Green Leaf understood the confusion in Dave's face and answered sincerely.

"My young friend. Long ago when kings ruled this land and the stories that you were told and grew up on were true. There came an evil that was intent on destroying all that was good and pure. All that breathed and lived it intended to destroy. You see, the Bad had one purpose, the taking of all life. Thankfully it was stopped by the power of friendship and beliefs. Dragons, faeries, elves, spooks and misfits of this world, came together under a banner of friendship and collaborated with the King of that time. An alliance was formed. We all fought side by side with the King, riding the backs of dragons and flying with the other faeries to confront the Bad."

Dave asked, "The Bad?"

"Yes. The Bad. This is the name that we have given to the evil that was attacking everything living. The army of myths, legends and folklore fought and defeated the Bad, but for one small living bit of it. The last remaining bit refused to die. It was taken away and buried deep down under the ground. A spell was cast to keep it imprisoned for good."

It all seemed unbelievable to Dave, but the unbelievable was flying around him. He continued to listen.

"That spell was based on how strong the beliefs of man was. Sadly as time has gone on, truths became mere stories and the spell that was cast has slowly weakened."

"And the storm?" Dave asked.

"The storm has nearly destroyed the tree completely. We had to place a spell to protect it from any more damage but, I must stress, that the spell is only temporary. We really don't know what to do at this moment." Elder Dandelion Green Leaf's voice softened, as if not having the answers to future forcible problems.

Everyone went silent as if accepting the inevitable, then Solomon said, "There must be something we can do."

Elder Swallowtail came forward and simply said, "Believe."

106

Dave stood there looking all around. Watching the mythical, legendary, childish stories that he was so engrossed with and interested in when he was a small boy. They were floating, fluttering and zipping about right in front of him. It was fantastical, unbelievable, magical and simply real all at the same time.

He started to remember that when he read stories of these mythical creatures, he so wished to see them, meet with them and play with them. Now his wish had come true.

Solomon, who was still playing joyfully with Zeal, Balamore and Caitlin, shouted his father over to join them in the playful fun.

Dave walked over to his son and was encouraged to kneel down and say hello to the badgers, foxes and a couple of magpies that had joined the group.

Meanwhile, Winnie was loving the moment also, for it had been a long time since an outsider had been given such special attention such as this.

Dave was stroking the badgers who were loving the attention, as well as the foxes who decided to rub their faces across Solomon's face. The feeling of beautiful silky smooth fur was an indescribable pleasure for the two of them. At the same time the two magpies perched themselves on Solomon and Dave's shoulders squawking out loud.

Dave remembered he had a box full of sandwiches that Sarah had made for them. He pulled them out and equally shared them with the animals and faeries. They were most grateful for the food.

A few faeries fluttered over and gave all the animals a few other tit bits that Winnie had brought

Winnie walked over accompanied by a few elders and said to Dave, "Something has to be done about the tree."

Dave got up and looked at Winnie, "I don't know what to do. If the only way of keeping the Bad locked away is getting people to believe, then it seems an impossible task."

He started to think hard then said, "Unless the faeries just presented themselves to everyone."

There was a little mumbling and an, "Impossible," from

one of the elders.

Zeal sprang up and said to everyone, "At least we have two more that believe. Every little bit of hope helps."

Elder Green Leaf smiled at that and knew Zeal was right. At the same time, Balamore smacked Zeal's shoulder as to say, "Well done."

Dave had a million questions to ask but didn't know where to start. There was one that he had always wanted to know the answer to.

"Why do you shine?" he asked.

With a smile on his face Elder Swallowtail answered, "Just like the firefly of the woodland we have the natural ability to shine. We are born with that ability, the gift of shine."

Dave's face shone just like the faeries were.

Elder Swallowtail continued.

"At birth our parents choose our colour, usually according to our name. In time we can change it. It's difficult but possible. Very few do."

Zeal jumped into the conversation, "Changer can."

"Changer?" Dave asked.

"Yes, Changer." Zeal answered, "That's not his real name, but we all call him Changer as for some reason he can change his colour instantly. Any colour. From blue, pink, red, white to black. Any colour. Really cool if you are playing hide and seek," then Zeal flew off.

He had another question, "Are you all this small?"

Elder Swallowtail had to smile at the curiosity of one who didn't believe until a few moments ago.

"No. We choose to be small as it helps conceal ourselves from the outside world. But in truth, we can change to any size we wish. Again, it takes time to learn and master. If I think it I could be your size."

Dave shook his head, still finding it difficult to believe what was going on. He looked at his watch and knew it was time to go. He didn't want to leave but it was getting to be the time to go back and have lunch with Sarah.

"Come on Solomon," he said, knowing that Solomon didn't

want to leave, which was understandable.

Solomon grumbled a little but after Caitlin gave him a kiss and a few words of friendship, he got up, held onto his father's hand and waited to go.

Winnie placed a hand on Dave's shoulder and said to him, "We are all in this together."

The badgers and foxes trundled away and the magpies flew to a nearby tree.

Elder Swallowtail flew over to Dave and Solomon and kindly said to them, "You will always be welcome here. Whenever you come we will greet you."

Dave and Solomon looked happily surprised.

Elder Swallowtail continued, "Please remember to come on your own and don't tell anyone about us. No-one will believe you."

Solomon and Dave agreed, but did ask if Sarah could be convinced, would she be allowed to come. They were told, "Yes." but only Sarah.

The two of them said goodbye to everyone. Winnie went with them and on the way home discussed with Dave what might happen in the future.

"You see, Dave," Winnie said, "it may seem like a dream, or even a faery tale, but if that thing that has been imprisoned for a thousand years escapes, it will mean the end of everything that we live for."

To Dave it did seem like a faery tale. One minute you are socialising with mystical creatures you were told could never exist, and then the next minute you are told that all life on this world could disappear if a terrible evil escapes.

Eventually, the three of them arrived at the garden of Dave and Solomon's house.

"Would you like to come in?" Dave asked.

"No thank you." Winnie answered, "I must contact the others in the village who know about what's going on, and see if we can come up with a plan."

Winnie said goodbye and was gone, travelling down another makeshift path that went through the wood.

Dave and Solomon just stood at the little steps that led onto their garden.

"Right Solomon," Dave said, "not a word to your mother, until I can figure out how to bring this whole thing up."

"Okay, Dad," Solomon said.

Dave picked up Solomon and helped him up and over the steps. Dave followed. They both walked down the path of the garden and into the house.

Way back in the wood, a pair of eyes was watching and these were not friendly.

"Ha, I see you. I know my master will be very happy."

The eyes of the little beast broke away and off it went back into the wood to contact its master. The Bad.

Dave and Solomon walked into the kitchen and Sarah was there, placing lasagne she had just made into the oven.

"Hello you two, great timing. I'm cooking lasagne," Sarah said.

Solomon's excitement was all over his face.

"Did you two have a good time in the wood?" Sarah asked.

"Mum! Mum! Me and Dad have been in the wood and have been playing with faeries, badgers, foxes and magpies. I was feeding them with some bread that Winnie gave me, and, and..." Solomon started to speak faster and faster.

"Hold on, hold on," Sarah said raising a hand as to stop Solomon from flying forward.

"What are you talking about?"

Dave stepped forward and gave Solomon a little kick with his foot, and said quietly, "Toe rag."

Solomon giggled.

Sarah looked at Dave and asked, "So, what did you two really do in the wood?"

"*This is going to be a little difficult,*" thought Dave.

With a cup of tea in one hand and a wild crazy story in the other, he thought he would give it a try and tell Sarah what he, and Solomon had seen and done in the wood.

After about 10 minutes, Sarah let out a loud laugh and said to Dave, "You nearly had me fooled. That's funny."

Solomon didn't think it was funny and went off upstairs in a huff. Dave understood and tried to keep calm. Inside he felt the same as Solomon did. He wanted the whole world to know. He felt he was going to explode having to keep the secret in. He was about to say something else when the phone rang. Sarah got up and still laughing she answered it. It was her mother just ringing to see how things were.

Dave knew that it was best to leave the story alone for another time, when Sarah was more calm and relaxed. Just then Dave looked through the patio doors that led out onto the garden.

He saw two birds hopping on the grass. Squinting his eyes, he couldn't believe what he was seeing. He was sure that the two birds were the two magpies that had been so friendly in the woods.

He stood up. Sarah was still chatting on the phone unaware what was happening outside in the garden.

As he walked closer to the patio doors he could see something on the back of one of the birds. It was shiny, glowing and glistening as the rays of the sun shone on it. He opened the patio doors and slowly walked out, quietly as not to scare the birds. Rather than being scared, the birds seemed joyful expressing delight at seeing him.

The two magpies hopped over to get closer to Dave. Without thinking, he raised his arm out and the two birds jumped up and perched themselves on his arm. Dave's face was one of deep surprise.

"Oh my goodness!" he exclaimed.

Now he could see what was shiny on the back of one of the magpies.

It was a shiny blue stone. When Dave looked at it the colours seemed to move on their own.

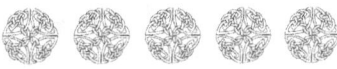

The little figure that watched Dave and Solomon walk home, flew to the old tree that was now encased by a cover of white light. The little creature flew very close to the tree, but not close enough that it could touch it.

"Master," it said, "I have found one that you can take as your own."

From beneath the tree there came a noise, more of a rumble because the ground shook ever so slightly.

This brought a smile on the little creature's face.

"It will be soon, very soon. I will bring the human to you then you can take him for yourself."

The creature spoke with a voice of deception and wore a smug face. Its heart was black and its ambitions were cruel, for it wanted power to rule, to rule over all those that lived in the wood and to take revenge on those that it didn't like, namely the faeries of the wood.

The ground shook again as if agreeing to the words that were being spoken. Then the little creature flew away.

After the magpies had delivered the stone they flew back to the wood. Dave ran past Sarah who was still on the phone, up the stairs and into Solomon's room. He saw his son crossed legged sitting on the floor, busily drawing everything he had experienced in the wood that very morning. After rushing into the bedroom, Dave hurriedly walked to Solomon and sat down next to him holding something in his hand.

Dave excitedly said, "Solomon!"

He looked up and answered, "Yes, Dad."

Dave then told Solomon about his encounter with the two magpies in the back garden. Solomon's face lit up.

"Look at my hand."

He looked at his father's hand and Dave opened it.

Solomon's bedroom was instantly illuminated by the swirling colours of the stone. It was like someone had switched on a very powerful torch, only this torch was no bigger than a fifty pence piece. The whole room became one gigantic light show of different colours.

Dave slowly placed the stone on the floor and the light

narrowed itself to a beam of light, that shone straight up spreading itself all across the ceiling of the bedroom. The light was dancing in all colours. Reds, blues, indigos, violets, purples, greens, gold and silver. It was mesmerising to watch. Then the light dimmed slightly and a voice came from the stone. It was the voice of Caitlin.

"My friends," the voice echoed though the room bouncing off all the walls, and into the very hearts of Solomon and Dave.

"This stone you have comes from a special place called the circle of friendship. And this stone will help you call for help whenever you need it. Whenever you are in need of help or in danger, use it."

The two of them just kept looking at the stone and listening to the enchanting voice.

"If you show it to anyone outside your immediate family, it will simply remain an ordinary looking stone. But, when either of you look at it together or on your own, it will come alive just as it is now. If you need help just call my name and I, or another faery will come to help you."

The light dimmed and the stone like Caitlin said, turned into an ordinary looking stone.

Dave looked at Solomon and said to him, "Now Solomon, you must keep this in a very special place."

Solomon thought about it and knew exactly where to put it. He got up and grabbed his best friend Rupert. He opened Rupert's jumper and placed the stone inside.

Dave smiled and thought, "*Great place!*"

When Winnie said goodbye to Dave and Solomon, she made her way back home. When she arrived home, the first thing she did was to call up the few people that knew about the secret in the wood. She called them to organise a meeting so she could tell them exactly what had happened. After she finished speaking to them, she placed the phone down and walked into the kitchen. She started to do something that she had done for a long time. She prepared food for the creatures of the wood.

As the day was drawing to a close, all the creatures in the wood were preparing themselves for a night's sleep except those that were nocturnal.

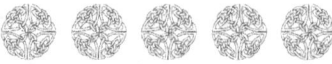

Back in the wood the owls had agreed to take watch for the night, guarding the tree and report immediately anything out of the ordinary. Owls can always be trusted and were very keen on taking the watch to help protect the wood and all that lived in it.

As well as the owls, a few foxes and badgers were keeping watch on the ground. They would smell anything strange before seeing it. Their acute sense of smell was invaluable. A small number of faeries decided to keep the foxes and badgers company also.

Zeal White Oak, Balamore Skullcap, a young faery called Geraldine Gooseberry and Sup Sup Rose chose to stay with the animals. All of these creatures watched the wood until the sun started to rise and the moon went to rest.

In the morning, Winnie was up early as usual and the food she had left out the previous night was all gone. She was getting ready to go out and see some friends in the village, to talk to them about what had happen and what may happen. The first person she went to see was Mrs Angela Dabner Crowner.

Mrs Angela Dabner Crowner owned and ran the local newsagents in the village. A thin looking woman, she always had her silver coloured hair tied up and wore round spectacles, which were held round her neck by a shoe lace tied to each arm. Whenever any news or message needed passing on, she was the right one to go to.

Winnie walked in and was greeted by Mrs Crowner with a

hearty, "Hello!"

Winnie replied back with an equally hearty, "Hello."

Angela asked, "What can I do for you."

"Well..." Winnie started her story, by telling Angela about Solomon and Dave and them being the latest of the small number of villagers who know about the faeries, "...so now they know and they have seen the tree, which is in no good shape at all."

The shop assistant appeared and Mrs Crowner asked her to take over the shop, while she took Winnie upstairs for a cup of tea, a slice of home made chocolate cake and more news about the impending danger.

As Winnie was telling more of the story and details of how terribly bad the tree was, both women suddenly felt a strange presence come over them. Like a slow gush of wind that creeps up to you from behind. The strange thing was that the two of them were indoors with all the windows shut and locked. The two women walked over to the biggest window in the room and peered out onto the village street.

The street was quiet, but for a rustling noise that was passing through. Winnie and Angela noticed the hedgerows and flowers in the front gardens of houses were wafting from side to side.

On the mornings TV weather report, there was no mention of wind or any bad weather. The two of them instead of keeping their eyes on the street, raised them up to the sky. Hearing a loud whooshing noise, both of the women ducked and saw on the street a huge shadow. Another and another. In fact, there were five shadows moving along the street, each bigger than a red double decker bus flying over houses and towards Birchover wood.

Both Winnie and Angela looked at each other, looked at the street and looked at each other again. As if they both knew what the other was saying, they both said out loud, "DRAGONS!"

"I must leave at once and see to my garden," Winnie said to Angela.

"I too," Angela replied.

"First, I'll spread the word to the rest of the group that the time of secrets has come to an end."

115

Winnie nodded and off she went, leaving thirty five pence on the counter for the paper she had picked up. On the front page, the headline was.

'GNOMES, ELVES AND DRAGONS HAVE LANDED!'

"You couldn't be more right," Winnie mumbled as she left the shop and headed home to greet some of the creatures.

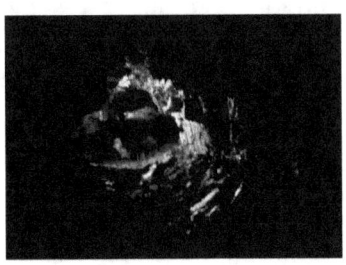

15

- TAKEN -

S arah, Dave and Solomon were out in the garden having a cup of tea and just talking. In Dave's mind, he was trying to work out when and how to tell Sarah of the magic inside the wood.

As they were all sitting down, a gush of wind blew past them nearly knocking all of them off their seats and onto the ground. They all stood up and looked around. As they did, the sun seemed to disappear and was replaced by a dark shadow. Looking down onto the grass, the three of them could see a huge shadow travelling along the ground and on towards the wood.

"What was that?" Sarah asked.

Dave had no idea, "Maybe a jet? Or a glider?" he said.

The three of them sat down, Dave looked at Solomon and Solomon looked at his dad.

"Er," Dave started, "Sarah, I think you better listen very carefully as to what Solomon and I have to say. It will seem a little unbelievable. But, I can assure you, it's the truth."

Sarah's face looked puzzled, but she was all ears.

Dave positioned himself comfortably on the chair, but just before he began to say something the three of them heard a noise.

From under a hedge came a sound of laughter. The three of them turned around and looked quickly to see what it was. As soon as they all turned their heads to see, all they saw was a movement of bushes and the thing that made the noise was gone. Sarah sat down shaking her head, "What's going on today?"

She then looked back at her husband and waited for him to tell her what was going on.

Dave's immediate thoughts were, *"Here goes!"*

It took about 15 minutes for Sarah to realise that both her son and husband were not kidding.

Solomon dragged his mother into the front room and asked her to sit down.

He ran upstairs to get Rupert, who had been placed on the bed as if he was guarding the sacred stone. Solomon came running downstairs and in front of his mother, he held out his hand.

Sarah saw a stone and thought nothing of it. She looked at Dave and he said to her, "Just watch." Then the stone started to glow.

A mixture of blue, white and green colours filled the room. Sarah watched the colours flowing, encircling her. Solomon was getting excited and Dave was just simply amazed by it all. Sarah just sat there with her mouth wide open and speechless.

After a few minutes of the dazzling light show, Solomon closed his hand and placed the stone carefully into his trouser pocket. Sarah looked at both her husband and son, she had nothing to say. A tear was flowing down one side of her face and Dave just took her in his arms and cuddled her.

As Winnie was walking through the village to get to her home, she kept hearing a little laughter and a rustling of leaves from nearby hedgerows. Winnie had a big grin on her face, which said that she had a good idea what was making the noise.

She eventually got home and went straight out to the back of her garden. She stood in the middle of her beautifully cut grass.

A rustling noise was heard again, but this time it was from the side. Winnie turned to face it.

"Don't be shy, I'm a friend," Winnie said in a gentle voice.

She held out her hand, which had some bread on it. Within a few seconds something walked forward, but couldn't be seen. It was invisible! Winnie smiled from ear to ear knowing all too well what it was.

"Well, well, you've come a long way, haven't you?" Winnie said to the invisible creature.

As she bent down she felt her face being caressed softly. Then some more rustling noises from the bushes and Winnie knew that this little creature was not alone. She was surrounded and felt their presence and if that wasn't enough, they started to show themselves to her.

"How wonderful!" Winnie exclaimed, "Brownies."

Knowing they were there, she was recalling in her mind what knowledge she had of brownies.

"Invisible brown elves, known also as household goblins. They usually live in farmhouses and other buildings that dwell in the country."

Winnie's knowledge of myths, legends and folklore was rushing through her head.

"If you're friends with a brownie, they will go about doing labours for the house when you're asleep. Brownies are protective creatures and can become very attached to the family that they are helping. If the family moves away, the brownie will move with them. But if you mistreat a brownie badly, the brownie will vanish without a trace and never to be seen again."

Winnie just stood still, "Oh, I wish little Solomon was here now," she said.

"I'm so privileged to see you. It's true, isn't it, that typically only children, because of their innocent nature can only see brownies?"

The brownies were excited and showed themselves to Winnie, because they knew she is kind, gentle and very protective of the secret.

Over a dozen of them surrounded her, holding and kissing

her and being very kind as brownies can be.

After the loving affection was over, the first brownie to appear to Winnie made a noise and the others started to vanish.

"I know, I know where you must go," Winnie said, "Go now and safe journey."

With a cheeky smile, the first of the brownies, who was the last to disappear gave Winnie a big hug and a kiss, then disappeared. The only sign of its presence was the occasional rustling of grass and bushes as it passed through Winnie's garden and into the wood.

After asking Dave and Solomon if she could go to the woods, she was told it was okay.

The three of them had put on their Wellington boots, and started walking up the path of the garden. Sarah had no idea what to expect. After all, she had been told a fabulous story about creatures she had always believed to be only stories.

The three of them jumped over the steps and into the wood. Sarah just stopped for a moment and looked into the woodland wondering what lay ahead. Dave took her hand to reassure her that everything was okay.

Solomon took the lead and said to her, "Don't be afraid. It's amazing."

She smiled and then started to walk forward, following her son as he took charge of the expedition. This was the first time for Sarah since moving to the village that she had ventured into the wood, and as she was walking she was making a mental note of what would be great to sketch.

The deeper they walked into the wood, the more interesting it became for Sarah. The whole place seemed to take on a medieval look. The way the trees had formed, twisted and knotted. To Sarah the shapes were magnificent to look at. Huge beasts of wood sprouting out of the ground and reaching high into the sky.

The branches of the trees flexed their leaf covered fingers, so as to catch as much of the sun and rain and also took on the shape of being the biggest umbrellas in nature. The whole spectacle was wonderful to Sarah, she was enjoying every moment.

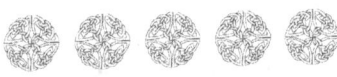

Back in the village, Angela was busy gathering the small number of locals that knew about the creatures of the wood. She was creating a plan of action, which would be needed when the time was right.

In the group there was, Arnold Simpson a local farmer. Cathy Brammall the florist of the village. Mavis Asher a local school teacher. Gerald Flewer a retired R.A.F pilot, and Cecilia Temmings who owned a few horses and a riding school.

Angela had told them what had happened with the tree, and how it was still protected but for how long was anyone's guess. She also told them about the new family that had moved into the village, and how the faeries had welcomed the father and son into the secret. The faeries were happy and confident that the family were good people.

After everything was discussed, the group waited for Winnie to get back and take over the meeting. Everyone knew without doubt, that Winnie was the most natural among the group when it came to communicating with the creatures of the wood. She seemed to understand them more than any other member of the group. If she was not at home, she was more likely than not to be in the wood where she would stay for hours and hours.

Winnie had decided to go into the wood and see what was happening. What she saw was something that even she never thought could have been possible.

Ahead of her were a group of female land nymphs. Beautiful and graceful. Nymphs love to sing and dance. These

121

nymphs were walking gracefully through the wood. One of them looked back and saw Winnie. She was walking slowly behind them not more than 30 feet, she was still mesmerised by their grace and beauty.

The nymph that looked smiled at Winnie showing no fear, but encouraged her to keep on going.

A few moments later and Winnie felt a vibration travelling through the floor of the wood. The sound seemed heavy and hard, completely the opposite to the way the nymphs were walking.

As she looked, she caught a glimpse of what was making the sound.

It wasn't one, but ten oakmen, tramping through the wood. They were in a hurry and not stopping for anything. Winnie couldn't believe her eyes. She was actually seeing walking trees!

She gradually made her way through the wood until she came to the circle. There she was met by some of the younger faeries, who swiftly told her that there was a meeting being held at a very special place called, the Nine Ladies Stone Circle.

Winnie followed the younger members of the faeries, who were zigzagging through the trees. She had to stop a number of times just to get her breath back, as the young faeries were moving at a rapid pace.

"I'm not as young as I use to be," she silently said to herself.

Eventually, Winnie got to the Nine Ladies Stone Circle, and what she saw was a magnificent, bewildering, spectacular sight that had not been seen for a very long time. Winnie pulled out a small mobile phone, called her friends and told them to get to the Nine Ladies Stone Circle as fast as possible. They had to see what she was seeing.

A mythical gathering of the oldest folklore creatures.

After taking their time walking through the wood, listening to the birds and admiring nature, eventually Sarah, Solomon and

Dave reached a part of the wood where the two of them could see a white light. This resembled the place they thought was the place of the tree.

Dave asked Sarah to move forward and when she did, she caught sight of the tree and the amazing vibrant white light that covered it.

"Is...Is that what I think it is?" Sarah asked.

Dave and Solomon smiled at each other, and stood beside her to give her support in case she was going to faint.

"Wait till you get up close," Dave said.

The three of them walked further into the wood, getting closer with every foot step they took until they stood in the presence of the white glowing tree.

The tree itself stood tall and proud even with the veil of white magic around it. The three of them stood in front of it, just a few feet away from the glowing bark. The pulsing white light looked beautiful, but something that was not meant to be touched.

"How? What? Is this for real?" was all Sarah could say at that time.

"Isn't it beautiful?" Dave said.

Solomon just looked with wide eyes and an open mouth.

"But why?" Sarah asked, not taking her eyes away from the light that housed a hidden danger.

Dave looked at Sarah, "For our protection. To keep what is underneath from escaping."

It was then Sarah looked at Dave. Her eyes said she wanted to know more, and wanted to see the faeries that had befriended her husband and son.

"Surely the thing that they are keeping buried must be dead by now?" she said.

Still looking at Sarah, Dave gently placed his hands around her face.

"Sarah," his voice was very slow and quiet, "The faeries said that we must never underestimate the power of the thing that's buried under that tree."

Sarah stroked Dave's face at the same time smiling. It was a difficult thing to believe, but now that Dave said it and believed it then she would to.

"Mum, Dad," Solomon was yanking his father's hand, "let's try and find our friends."

Dave looked at his son, "Good idea Solomon."

The three of them turned away from the tree and as they did, a little light came from behind it and whizzed towards them.

Solomon sensing something turned his head around.

"Mum. Dad. Look!" Solomon said jumping with excitement.

The moving light was a faery, and one they had not seen before.

The little creature flew over and hovered above Solomon's head. It glowed brightly. It was only until the faeries glow died down that they could see the face.

The faeries glow was one of a light brown colour, and he was no more the size of Solomon's hand. He fluttered over to Sarah and Dave and introduced himself.

"Hello everyone. I am Cowl Monkshood. I've come here to help you."

Sarah looked at the faery in amazement. Everything Dave and Solomon said was true! Little people did exist and there was one right in front of her face. Sarah was speechless.

Cowl Monkshood looked at Solomon, "You must be Master Solomon. I've heard so much about you."

Solomon's face beamed with a smile. He felt like he was famous.

Cowl Monkshood fluttered down close to Solomon and looked at him carefully. With inspecting eyes he said to Solomon, "Er, yes. You will do nicely," he then fluttered to one side of Solomon and said to all three of them.

"Follow me. We must go past the tree and deeper into the wood. Follow me, follow me."

Solomon, Dave and Sarah turned and walked closer to the tree, doing exactly what Cowl Monkshood told them to do. Solomon was in front, with Sarah in the middle and then Dave behind. Solomon was fiddling with his little stone that was in his pocket. It felt a little warmer than normal and seemed to be glowing. Glowing so much, that some of the light started to briefly shine through the tightly woven strands that made up his pocket of his pants.

Sarah saw it first, "What's that?" pointing at the beams of red and yellow light that were just about penetrating Solomon's pants and coat.

Dave saw it as well and moved forward.

As he did, Cowl Monkshood fluttered over to Solomon and in between Sarah and Dave.

"It's nothing. It's nothing!" Cowl Monkshood said in a hissing tone, while trying to keep Solomon separated from his parents. He was now slowing edging Solomon closer to the tree.

Just then another light came through the wood. It was Caitlin!

She saw what was happening and flew as fast as she could to Dave and Sarah.

Seeing Caitlin got Cowl Monkshood worried and irritable.

Caitlin hovered by the shoulder of Dave and demanded to know what was going on.

"Go back. Go BACK!" the panic stricken faery shouted. Solomon was getting a little scared. "You have no right to be here!" he screamed at Caitlin.

Caitlin quickly said to Dave, "Solomon is in danger. Whenever Solomon or a family member is in danger, the stone will shine red and yellow."

Dave had a look of worry on his face.

Caitlin moved forward to Solomon but Cowl Monkshood was too quick. With all his strength he pushed Solomon closer to the tree.

"What are you doing?" Caitlin demanded.

"Something that should have been done a long time ago." Cowl Monkshood waved his arms in the air, and saliva fell from his mouth as to show his distaste to the intrusion and questions. "I have been watching this family. This boy has been chosen to be the host."

"What are you saying?" Caitlin screamed out, "Host! What host?"

"What I am saying is, this boy will be the host for my new master."

Just then, Zeal and Balamore came rushing through the trees and floated by the side of Caitlin, Dave and Sarah.

"Not even the heroic Zeal or Balamore can save the boy now." Cowl Monkshood sarcastically shrieked out.

"Don't be a fool!" Zeal said, "Whatever the problem is, we can work it out."

"Huh! You may have been the heroes at the battle of Grin Low, but you will not be here. Too late for you. Too late for all of you. You will soon feel the power of my new master."

To the disbelief of all who were watching, and before Solomon could cry out to his parents, Cowl Monkshood grabbed and yanked Solomon towards the tree. The moment the two of them touched the tree, they vanished.

Caitlin, Zeal, Balamore, Dave and Sarah looked on in astonishment.

One moment Solomon was there, the next he was gone sucked into the heart of the tree.

Sarah let out a scream and fell into Dave's arms.

Looking at Sarah and then looking at the tree, Dave was lost for words and couldn't fully understand what had just taken place.

After a few moments he looked at the three faeries who held their heads down.

"What's happening?" Dave demanded.

Zeal flew over to Dave, "You and your wife must follow us, to a place called the Nine Ladies Stone Circle."

"We're not going anywhere until our son is back with us." Dave shouted.

"Please," Caitlin pleaded, "the elders will have the answers."

16

- THE GATHERING -

Winnie was standing by some trees on the edge of the Nine Ladies Stone Circle. In front of her she could see a magical gathering.

It was a spiritual presence of mythical creatures. Myths, legends and folklore.

Surrounding the circle were dragons, five of them, all looking like they were made of gold! The leader of this group of dragons was called Gerth.

Next to them were the oakmen, with hundreds of portunes sitting on their branches. There were also boggarts, derricks, knockers and brags, as well as the faeries led by the elders. A few of the faeries flew over to Winnie and told her not to be afraid of these creatures. All of the gathering had one thing in common and that was to protect everything that is living.

Winnie was invited to mingle among the creatures and after a little persuasion, she accepted. Slowly she walked over and was introduced to the group by Elder Perennial Swallowtail.

"My dear friends, I would like to introduce to you a very good and trusted friend of the faeries. Her name is Winnie. Winnie Tucker of the human folk."

There was a sound that could only be described as a mixture of happiness and laughter. It was very loud. The first one to speak from the group of extraordinary creature's, was Gerth. The dragon.

"Welcome, dear Winnie."

His voice was gentle and kind in sound, but his size was commanding. He had a look of royalty. Winnie didn't know what to do but managed to smile.

"Ha, ha," Gerth let out, "Don't be afraid of our kind. We will do you no harm. A friend of the faeries is a friend of ours for life."

With a gentle flip of his huge tail, Gerth pushed Winnie closer to him so that she could feel she was part of the group. After that, every creature introduced him, her or itself to Winnie.

This exciting time was then looked upon by Winnie's friends who had rushed through the wood. The friends of Winnie nearly collapsed at the sight of the gathering. It wasn't until Winnie came to them and excitedly introduced everyone that they started to feel more at ease once they quickly got accustomed to the extraordinary sight.

It was a time of rejoicing. Old friends had been reunited. All the creatures were talking in their own tongues. They were all talking together, reminiscing about the old days. Their facial expressions conveyed great happiness and joy.

After a while, when everyone had greeted one another, the group allowed the true reason they were back to spoil the happy, joyful atmosphere. It was a sad day for they had all been summoned because of a great evil.

Back in the days when the King of England fought along side such great beasts to defeat the Bad, a magical pact was formed, so that if at any time the Bad was ever to find a way to escape from the tree, then the spirits of myth, legends and folklore would come back and fight once again side by side, to protect the innocent. It was their duty. Their solemn vow. It was now the time to fulfil that promise.

One of the creatures, an oakman introduced himself.

"A good day to you, my dear lady. Some call me old tree

man, but I don't feel old and I don't think I am old. My full name is so long and difficult in your language you can call me..." The oakman paused trying to think of an easy name to be called by. He tilted his head slightly, looking up at the blue sky and as if a wonderful thought had just popped into his head, his whole face seemed to smile. Looking at Winnie he said.

"It is what I am and what I will always be, I would like to be simply called, Tree."

The oakman rocked a little from side to side as is he was chuckling. He then asked Winnie and her friends how they were remembered.

Angela Crowner spoke up, "Sadly, you're only remembered in stories, children's books and bed time tales," she quickly thought about what she had just said and felt that she had said the wrong thing.

"Wonderful!" Tree rejoiced out loud, "To be remembered in stories. To be spoken about and passed on from adult to child, is indeed a wonderful thing."

Angela and her friends couldn't understand the happy tone in the voice of the oakman.

"I...I'm sorry. I don't understand." Angela said having a look of bewilderment. Winnie on the other hand, who was standing close to her understood perfectly.

"My dear," Tree said, "it is in every beasts wish, to have one's noble deeds written down and passed on from one generation to another. To be spoken of in such a way is honourable indeed."

That was when Angela and her friends understood what Winnie already knew. The myths, legends and folklore were in their own eyes not forgotten, but remembered alongside the great knights and kings of old.

Without warning, Zeal, Balamore, Caitlin, Dave and Sarah burst through the trees. All of them came face to face with the gathering that had assembled around the Nine Ladies Stone Circle. Both Dave and Sarah couldn't believe their eyes, but their faces told a different tale.

"Ha, more guests," Gerth shouted out loud. The huge gathering all looking in the direction of the new visitors.

Caitlin, Zeal and Balamore flew over to the elders who had congregated together. They told the elders what they had witnessed.

The faces of the elders looked very solemn. After hearing the news, Elder Swallowtail moved to the centre of the gathering and asked everything and everyone to listen to the news.

Zeal, Balamore and Caitlin, went back to Dave and Sarah to give them hope. Winnie was now next to them. Dave and Sarah were staring at the gathering.

"Now, don't you worry." Winnie said to them. She could see that Sarah was looking very distraught.

"Wh...What is this?" Dave asked trying to understand what was happening.

Winnie told him everything that she knew. She carefully explained to the two of them, since the first encounter with the evil, if ever the evil or the Bad presented itself at any time, then there would always be good to battle it. Today was that day.

Just then Dave heard a voice in his head. It was Elder Swallowtail calling him over to the circle. Dave told Sarah to relax and that he had to go to speak with the elders.

Sarah was still shaking a little, but after a little sip of herbal tea that one of the faeries made and gave to her, she started to relax and was more focused.

Dave walked over and was kindly met by all the elders. He was surprised that they had changed their size to match his.

Elder Swallowtail was the first to come forward and greet him.

He asked Dave exactly what happened. All the elders listened carefully about how he, Sarah and Solomon were met by a faery called Cowl Monkshood. How the stone that Caitlin gave Solomon, started to shine at the moment Cowl Monkshood made Solomon walk closer to the tree.

Dave talked to them for several minutes until he finished his story. He could see on their faces they were concerned for Solomon and how serious the situation had become. Also, they were heart broken that one of their own had somehow been involved with the abduction of Solomon.

They quickly conveyed their utmost apologies to him.

"What is going to happen to Solomon?" Dave asked them.

"We have hope," Elder Perennial Swallowtail said.

"You see, the Bad has taken Solomon because he is young and most importantly, innocent. Innocent in mind and spirit. It wishes to take on the form of a human. The one thing you must do is believe that all hope is not lost."

Dave looked confused, "What do you mean hope is not lost?" Dave couldn't help but feel riled. "An evil has taken my son with the help of one of your own. How are you going to stop it? How is hope going to help?"

The elders felt and understood the pain he was going through. They also had also lost one of their own to the Bad.

"Master Dave." Elder Dandelion Green Leaf said, "There is hope, there is always hope when one looks for it. Solomon is innocent. His spiritual connection to his parents, to you and Sarah is very strong. It will take the love of both you and Sarah, to help Solomon and save him from the grip of the Bad."

Dave quickly composed himself and listened carefully, but couldn't help think about his son.

"Children have no conception of what evil is. That is the hope. It will be you and Sarah that will save Solomon. No-one else. The love you two have for him is strong. Between parent and child. No evil can break that. The love you have for your son is what will destroy the Bad. If the Bad loses Solomon, then it will lose the power to live and will finally die."

The words of Elder Dandelion Green Leaf were re-assuring to Dave and he still trusted the faeries. Dave asked one more question.

"What must I do?"

17

- THE BAD -

Solomon and Cowl Monkshood found themselves in a large cave as soon as they touched the tree. Solomon was making a mumbling, whimpering sound and was ready to cry.

"STOP!" Cowl Monkshood demanded and Solomon quickly did as he was told.

"I must take you to my master. Move."

With incredible strength, Cowl Monkshood pushed Solomon through a labyrinth of tunnels that were formed under the wood. As he was being pushed, Solomon could see that the roots of trees were jutting through the sides and ceiling of the tunnels he was walking through.

Some of the roots were so long that Solomon had to duck down so to avoid hitting his head.

Cowl Monkshood didn't care, he kept pushing Solomon

through the tunnels and Solomon didn't know where he was going.

"You're not like a proper faery." Solomon said to Cowl Monkshood.

"Shut up you little brat!" Cowl Monkshood scowled at Solomon, "Anyway, how would you know what a faery should be like?"

"Caitlin, she showed me." Solomon said, "She told me what faeries do for people. You are nothing like her, or her friends. You're just a coward."

Feeling a little a brave he pulled out his tongue at Cowl Monkshood.

"All that is about to change. Your so called wonderful friends won't save you now. Everyone will bow to their new master soon. They will show me the respect I rightly deserve. I will rule over the faeries."

"Why? What have they done to you?" Solomon had to ask.

Cowl Monkshood pulled Solomon to a grinding halt. Looking at him with crazy, flaming eyes he said, "What have they done to me? It's what they haven't done. Never have they appreciated my talents. Never have they looked at me and thought that I should be an elder of the order. Menial jobs I was given."

Solomon felt he was being pushed and pulled as Cowl Monkshood was vexing his anguish on him.

"Help with nest building. Clear the leaves. Check to see if there is enough food for the animals. Blah! I was born to be a warrior. Not a SERVANT!"

The last word was said with such anger, the sound bounced of the walls and seemed to hurt Solomon's ears. Lose soil fell from the ceiling of the tunnel, being disrupted by the ferocious noise.

"But, maybe they were doing that to teach you, before you could be a warrior?" Solomon said trying to ease the situation.

The faery looked at Solomon with disgust and spat at him.

"You human. You don't know a thing. Nothing! But there was one who promised me many years ago. Promised me power and glory. All I had to do was stop Elder Perennial Swallowtail from engaging in the big battle at Grin Low Woods. That master is no-more. I have a new and more powerful one. It will give me what I want."

Cowl Monkshood got tired of talking, and pushed Solomon again through the tunnel until they arrived at a huge opening, which was as big as a football field. Cowl Monkshood pushed Solomon until they were about in the centre of the vast open chamber.

"Now we wait," his voice echoed through the open space.

Solomon noticed that throughout his journey, everything was lit by what looked like diamonds or glass stones. Theses diamond like objects were embedded into the wall of the tunnel, reflecting Cowl Monkshood's light and illuminating the surrounding area as they walked.

The place he was standing in was no different. Hundreds or maybe thousands of diamond like stones, were in the walls of the chamber and all helped to light up the open space.

Solomon looked at Cowl Monkshood and said to him, "My dad is going to get me and when he does, you'll be in big trouble."

Cowl Monkshood smiled then laughed. A cold and sinister sound came out from his little mouth.

"You really think that don't you, Solomon? I have news for you. No one is coming for you. Not now. Not ever."

He continued to laugh, the chilling sound bouncing off the walls of the open space.

"Those petty fools are just waiting for the obvious. Their own destruction."

As Cowl Monkshood was basking in his own egotistical, delusional glory, there was nothing in his actions that showed he was once part of a kind and caring community of faeries. A mythical group of beings that had helped him, taught him and loved him.

As Solomon was watching Cowl Monkshood, something was stirring in the background of the cave. To the back of the faery was the thing that he was waiting for.

A noise stopped Cowl Monkshood from continuing in his self-obsessed magnificence. The vibrations from the noise started to shake Solomon.

At first the noise started quietly, then rose to a loud

shrieking pitch before dying down again.

Cowl Monkshood flew behind Solomon and with fear in his voice, he said, "Master. Here he is as promised. This young boy. Solomon is your vessel for leaving this prison, so that you can take revenge once and for all. You can now end your torment forever."

The thing that made the noise now showed itself to Solomon.

It was a few feet away when Solomon could just make out a shape.

It was about the size of a small dog and it slithered like a snake. As it slimed around where Solomon stood, Solomon kept turning around watching it, tracking it to see what it would do next. He noticed that occasionally, the thing would stretch out what looked like black gooey tentacles. They would feel the ground, then the body would jump forward and suck the tentacles back into its slimy, gooey body. It did this until it had fully slithered a path around where Solomon was standing.

The light that Cowl Monkshood projected illuminated the Bad.

Solomon could see what it looked like. The thing was as black as oil and as slimy as a slug. It gave Solomon a terrible feeling.

When the Bad stopped moving, it was still at the base of Solomon's feet. It looked like a black puddle. Solomon tried to step backwards but Cowl Monkshood was behind him and pushed Solomon a little more forward.

As Solomon was forced to move forward, the black slimy thing jumped up in to the air. For a few moments it seemed to hover over Solomon's head. Solomon looked up at it and before he could make a sound, the black thing dropped onto his face smothering him, covering his face completely.

After a minute it had covered him from head to toe. Solomon looked like a black statue covered in oil. Unlike oil, this thing was alive.

A noise of gulping echoed throughout the chamber as if the thing was swallowing the poor boy whole.

Cowl Monkshood smiled gleefully. He was unprepared for

what was about to happen next.

Without warning, a tentacle of black slime shot out and grabbed Cowl Monkshood. He tried to struggle to get out of the grip but couldn't break free.

"Wh...What are you doing, Master?" he yelped.

"I need your magic." came a chilling dark voice.

Cowl Monkshood was trapped, "But, I've helped you. I've served you with loyalty," he screamed out.

"Yes, you have. Now you can serve me with loyalty one last time," the voice replied.

With no time to scream, Cowl Monkshood was sucked into the blob of black slime that had covered Solomon. A few seconds later, Cowl Monkshood had been completely sucked in and was gone.

Solomon's body started to shake and a white glow started to appear around the black slime. The two things the Bad needed that would give it the strength to escape were now joined together. A human child and faery magic.

The glow grew brighter and brighter, until it was as bright as the sun. Beams of light shot out in different directions and as quick as the light shone, it disappeared leaving just blackness. The cold blackness of the chamber took over.

A few minutes passed and light came back to the vast empty cave. The black slime was gone and all that stood was Solomon. He was different, very different.

With a faint glow still surrounding him, Solomon smiled, stretched out his arms, gave a big yawn then opened his eyes.

Instead of the eyes of a young, energetic, vibrant young boy, the eyes were black as the darkness that surrounded him. The Bad had taken Solomon over. It needed a physical body and Solomon was chosen for that purpose.

As for Cowl Monkshood, he was gone never to come back.

Solomon, who was now taken completely over by the Bad, started to walk out of the vast cave and through the tunnels. As Solomon walked everything behind him started to cave in. Tunnels filled up with falling earth. There was no more need for this prison. Everything behind was disappearing. The earth was swallowing everything up.

This continued until Solomon stood under a large area where, thick twisted roots appeared.

Solomon looked up. He saw the roots from the tree that held the Bad for a thousand years. It was only a matter of a few moments, before the Bad would taste the fresh air of the English countryside and start its journey of destruction once again.

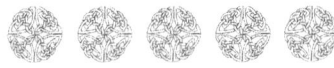

The gathering had increased in numbers since the magical creatures came to help.

Foxes, badgers, hundreds and hundreds of mice. Otters, ravens, crows, owls and every other woodland bird and creature there was. Everything and everyone that had heeded the call for help, turned up. The gathering was an amazing sight for all to see and a heart warming one.

During the time the humans were getting to know all the myths, legends and folklore, Winnie gave Tree a new name.

She explained that as we all refer to his kind as trees, a dedicated name would be more appropriate. Tree agreed happily and was extremely excited, impressed and honoured when Winnie named him Autumn Brown Leaf.

After the naming of Tree, Elder Perennial Swallowtail quickly took charge and ordered those who could fly, to take to the skies and those who were on foot to head for the trees.

"Our battle starts and ends in the wood," he shouted, "We start at the tree."

Everyone and everything knew which tree he was talking about. After that, the huge majestic dragons led by Gerth took to the skies, followed by all the birds and a large number of eagles and falcons that had just arrived. On foot, everything else charged forward led by the faeries, followed by the oakmen who kindly picked up Winnie and her friends, Dave and Sarah.

After the oakmen, everything else moved on towards the tree.

After a while and with a crashing of voices stampeding through the wood, everything that was at the gathering stopped walking. Everything that was flying perched itself on trees. Four dragons just gracefully circled above the wood with Gerth landing. Everything had arrived at the oldest tree in the wood.

Thousands of eyes looked and stared at the tree that was still glowing with white light. It all looked peaceful and secure. The elders and especially Elder Swallowtail, could feel something was wrong. He knew something was about to happen.

He shouted to everyone, "PREPARE YOURSELVES!"

Something did happen, which instantly scattered all the birds in to the air.

Without warning, the ground of the wood started to vibrate and shake like an earthquake.

Autumn Brown Leaf yelled, "The Bad. I can feel it. IT'S COMING!"

Everything and everyone steadied themselves and looked at the tree. The glowing light faded in and out like it was losing power. After a few seconds the light disappeared completely. Everyone and everything saw the tree as it really was, and what damage was caused from the great storm. Everything went quiet as still as the night.

The old tree had secured and kept the Bad imprisoned for a thousand years. It had been a beacon of strength and a place for the dying. Now it looked battered and worn after it had been hit by the lightning strike.

Without a sign or a sound, the tree erupted in a flash of light then exploded.

The ancient oak tree blew apart. Tree bark and wood flew in all directions. Smoke erupted into the air forming a white and black mushroom cloud. Yells, cries and screams came from the beasts of the wood.

At first, all that could be seen was bark and branches of the old oak lying on the ground. More and more of the damage could be seen as the smoke began to disappear.

Through the soil of the wood, a vibration could be felt and a slight humming sound could be heard. A few moments passed and the noise settled down. The smoke from the explosion disappeared and everything saw what was left. A huge oak tree split into four pieces.

The four pieces of oak tree lay on the ground, pointing in four separate directions. A huge hole was now in the middle where the base of the tree stood. Everyone waited to see what would happen next. Gerth was the first to speak.

"Let me bring fire down upon that, which has not yet appeared."

Elder Perennial Swallowtail held up his hand. Gerth went quiet. Just then the thing that Elder Swallowtail was waiting for, happened.

Solomon, which was now the Bad appeared slowly from beneath the ground. Up through the hole and floated in the middle of the split tree.

"SOLOMON!" cried out Dave and Sarah.

Solomon did not listen. He faced the ground with his hands by his side.

Everything and everyone gazed at the boy not knowing what to do.

He still looked like an innocent young boy.

Elder Swallowtail spoke knowing only too well what was hiding in the body of Solomon.

"DO NOT PLAY GAMES!" he shouted, "Show yourself."

Just as he was asked, Solomon raised his head and opened his eyes showing all that looked how black and evil they were.

There were noises of snarling and gnashing of teeth from the beasts ready for battle. Gerth growled at him. Everything and everyone that looked at the boy couldn't believe the evil was back.

Dave and Sarah were nearly in tears.

Just as before there came a laughter from the voice of the Bad. His smile showed contempt for all that were in the wood.

"I am here. FREE AT LAST!" A cold voice came from Solomon's lips.

"This time, I will not be stopped by some old fool who claimed to be King. Or by his feeble pawns. Especially by you, Elder Perennial Swallowtail."

The Bad looked at the dragons and raised Solomon's fist.

"OR BY SOME OLD WORTHLESS WEAK DRAGONS!"

That infuriated Gerth. The five dragons were riled. All five of them blasted a sound deep from within their chests. The sound was like a mountain splitting in two and the exploding sound of thunder.

One of the dragons flew down and swooped with the intentions to knock the monster over. The Bad raised Solomon's index finger of his right hand.

Blue and white electricity shot out and hit the dragon dead centre in its stomach. The dragon was knocked back spinning backwards as he was pushed up into the sky. He growled loudly, being surprised by the jolt rather than from the pain. What pain there was quickly disappeared. The dragon found its balance in the sky and rejoined the others.

Solomon looked at everyone else and laughed.

"My power is getting stronger every minute I am in this body," the Bad hissed.

"GIVE ME BACK MY SON!" shouted Sarah, who tried to run forward but was stopped by Dave.

The Bad looked at Sarah and to torment her even more, it said in Solomon's own voice, "Mother. Mother. HELP ME!" shrieking laughter followed.

"ENOUGH!" Elder Swallowtail shouted, "This ends here and it ends now."

Elder Swallowtail held out his hand and a ball of red light bolted out and hit Solomon dead centre in his chest. The impact sent the boy falling. He hit the soil of the wood and skidded for a few seconds.

As he lay there Elder Swallowtail shouted, "EVERYONE! YOU KNOW WHAT TO DO."

With that command, all the birds flew away and those on foot moved deeper into the wood.

The Bad stood up fuming with anger. As it looked around the whole area was empty.

"FOOLS!" the Bad screamed out.

Smoke was whirling around the scorched tree and the Bad

squinted its eyes.

It said in a low voice, "I will crush you all. Starting with you, Elder Swallowtail."

The Bad looked at its new body and was pleased with it. While it was revelling in its own grand self-admiration, it didn't notice something glowing in a small pocket of Solomon's trousers.

All the animals fled away in all directions under the orders of Elder Swallowtail.

Sarah, Dave and Winnie, as well as Winnie's friends were scooped up and carried away by the oakmen.

The Dragons were flying high, occasionally circling the wood and keeping a close eye on the Bad's whereabouts.

Everyone and everything had vanished into the wood waiting for the right time to appear.

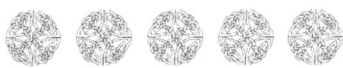

The Bad having control of Solomon was walking through the wood and heading upwards. The wood thick with trees, surrounded the Bad as it walked slowly wanting to get to higher ground, so as to see where it was and in what direction it wanted to start its takeover of this world.

Walking up to a fallen tree that was blocking its path, the Bad simply walked into it. It exploded, splitting it in two with both parts being blown away from each other. From the mist of falling wood chips and broken bark, walked the Bad. Through the gap of the exploded tree, it walked with a sinister smirk on its face, feeling the power of a thousand years slowly coming back. It felt invincible.

A few faeries had followed carefully where the Bad was going. They were all shocked after seeing the destruction of a tree. When the Bad was well clear of it, three faeries flew as fast as possible to the destroyed tree and looked at the damage.

One of the faeries called Knuckles Parsnip was glowing with anger. He had to be held back from taking on the Bad. If there was one thing that faeries hated the most, it was the unnecessary destruction of nature. One of nature's finest was the tree.

The smallest of the three, called Peach Bolder looked at the destroyed tree and said, "We must get back to the others and tell them what we have seen. They need to know where the Bad is going."

As quick as a flash the three of them flew away.

The Bad was still walking up through the wood, and was intent on getting to a part of the woodland that was clear. This would give it a clear view of its whereabouts.

Eventually, it got to the highest point of the woodland. It was now only surrounded by very young saplings.

It looked ahead and was able to make out the woods domain. Next it saw the village and then the surrounding road system.

High in the sky the five dragons glided still watching and waiting.

In the wood the Bad could see an occasional rustling of trees.

"Oakmen!" the Bad said in a voice of disgust, "When I get the chance, I'll burn every single one of them."

The Bad plotted its journey. It headed down back through the wood and towards the village. As it left the area, all the young saplings were on fire.

With everything and everyone scattered, it seemed that there was no hope but this was part of the plan.

Elder Perennial Swallowtail had given orders to make it seem that everyone had scattered away.

The dragons were in the sky to keep an eye on Solomon, who seemed to be completely under the control of the Bad. They were to report back everything he was doing.

The oakmen were to protect the humans and the rest of the beasts were preparing traps for the Bad.

Zeal, Caitlin and Balamore floated in-front of Elder Swallowtail.

"You know what to do," he said to the three of them.

"We do." the three of them answered and without being told, they immediately flew away.

Elder Perennial Swallowtail looked at the rest of the faery clan and they all nodded, knowing that it was their only chance if they were to defeat the Bad and save Solomon. They all flew off. He then looked at the oakmen.

"As well as looking after our new friends, you must try and get Solomon to follow you. I feel there is a part of Solomon that can still be reached and he will want to follow his parents. Where they go Solomon will follow. That and the Bad's hatred of trees."

The oakmen smiled. They knew that the Bad hated them.

Trees were and still are an integral part of life. Beasts of the wood need trees to live in during winter. The falling leaves provide food for the soil. The wood of the tree is used for construction. Trees help regulate the temperature of the Earth. They help disperse howling wind. They take away poisons from the air and replace it with new, fresh oxygen. They are the lungs of the Earth.

This is what the Bad hated. Life is reliant on a piece of wood.

Carefully holding Dave and Sarah, Autumn Brown Leaf and the rest of the oakmen walked deep into the wood to meet the Bad on their own territory.

In the mind of Elder Swallowtail and all the other elders, this plan had to work. If it failed it would mean the end of everything.

Zeal, Caitlin and Balamore rushed through the wood. Faster than they had ever travelled before. Their little wings beating at an incredibly fast speed. If you could have seen them, they would have past you within a blink of an eye. Only leaving you with a little buzzing sound and a trail of light as they past by.

The three of them flew as fast as their little wings could carry them. Zipping up and over trees, around branches and through holes in dead fallen tree trunks. Zeal held up an arm and the three of them slowed down, stopped and hovered. They could sense the evil of the Bad not far from them. They paused for a few moments then continued to fly, until Caitlin saw Solomon walking through the wood and towards the village.

Balamore said, "We have to do something before the oakmen arrive."

"I know," Zeal answered and as if he had suddenly gone crazy, he looked at both of his friends and said, "I'm going to talk to him."

Off Zeal went flying towards Solomon. Caitlin and Balamore knew instinctively what he was going to do and followed him.

The three were going to buzz around Solomon as fast as they could to try and slow him down. It was dangerous, but necessary.

Zeal was the first to fly in front of the Bad. Then came Caitlin followed by Balamore.

All three started to whiz round and around Solomon's head. The Bad tried to flick them away, but they were too fast.

"So you have come to intimidate me have you?" the Bad spoke, cold and unnatural was the sound of the voice. "Couldn't Swallowtail come. I see he doesn't have the guts to face me. Instead he sends his play toys to do his work."

Caitlin didn't like what was being said and quickly flicked the ear of Solomon.

The Bad reacted by trying to catch Caitlin, but again she was too fast.

Caitlin shouted, "You won't win."

The cold voice of the Bad laughed and it carried on walking. Zeal flew down to the back of Solomon, picked up a fallen branch and positioned it at the back of Solomon's head.

"Sorry Solomon," Zeal said in a quiet voice.

With all his strength he flew hard and fast, thrashing the branch at the back of Solomon's head and hitting the back and side of it.

"AAARRRRHHHHHH!" screamed the Bad.

144

A trickle of blood dribbled down the right side of Solomon's face from a small cut. Within an instant, the cut closed up and the blood dried in the morning sun.

"Right you little pests."

The Bad stopped walking and raised up his hands. With his palms facing up a red glowing light appeared. Floating above his palms a small round red object formed, which had the appearance of fire.

"See how you like a little heat, my pesky little friends."

Immediately, the Bad started to throw fireballs the size of footballs in all directions. As each one missed the faeries, each of the fireballs hit and exploded against trees.

Just missing a fireball that was heading his way, Balamore shouted to Caitlin and Zeal, "BE CAREFUL! We can't keep this up forever."

"And I thought repelling energy bolts at the cavern was difficult!" Zeal replied.

"It'll get a lot more difficult and hotter if we don't do something quick!" Caitlin added.

From above the wood in the sky the five dragons could see what was happening. Gerth, the leader of the dragons looked at one of the other dragons and shouted, "COOL HIM DOWN!"

The dragon that was told this just fell into a steep dive, as if he was a falling stone gaining speed from every second of the fall.

With his mouth open he started to suck in the air that was rushing past. Once he gathered enough air he tipped a wing and with incredible skill, entered the wood gliding only a few feet above the ground.

As he was getting closer to the Bad, who was still throwing fireballs, he shouted at Caitlin, Zeal and Balamore.

"My brave little friends. MOOOOOVVVVVEEEEEEE!"

Caitlin, Zeal and Balamore saw what was coming at them. A huge golden dragon!

Immediately, all three of them dashed to one side and hid behind a tree. As they did, the Bad spun around to face the dragon.

Looking at the Bad the golden dragon smiled.

With only 100 metres between the two of them and getting

closer, one huge burst of cold icy air shot from the dragon's nostrils covering Solomon from head to toe.

The dragon blew hard for about 10 seconds. For every second the dragon blew he got closer and closer to Solomon. Within a foot of colliding into him, the dragon stopped blowing and closed its mouth, and with incredibly skill and agility twisted its streamlined body to one side missing Solomon.

The iced covered Bad didn't move. Covered in a thick layer of ice, soil and leaves, which were whipped up from the ground as the dragon flew past. Solomon looked like an ancient statue.

The dragon flew back into the sky smiling, feeling proud that it had the chance to help out.

Solomon stood there frozen still. He was so cold that a fog of ice was blowing off his frozen body. There was no movement.

"Should we go and see?" Caitlin asked.

"NO!" exclaimed Zeal, "Just wait."

Zeal was right. After a few moments there was movement coming from under the body of ice that covered Solomon.

A cracking sound could be heard. Quiet at first but the sound then started to get louder. An eruption of sound then a thunderous explosion. Blocks of ice flew everywhere and some nearly hit the three faeries.

After the rain of ice had settled down, Solomon was standing there checking himself for any damage. He looked up at the sky after he had finished. Seeing the dragons he screamed a growl at them. The noise echoed throughout the wood. The dragons and the faeries saw the Bad starting to walk again in the direction of the village.

"We must do something," cried Caitlin.

"There's nothing we can do," Balamore said.

"We could combine our powers to slow him down," Zeal said to them.

Looking at each other, they agreed and flew ahead of Solomon to confront him.

In the sky the dragons roared in frustration. They weren't going to give up. The five of them kept on flying following the Bad.

Zeal, Caitlin and Balamore stopped a few hundred metres from Solomon. Floating side by side forming a straight line, they held each other's hands. Each of their colourful aurora glowed with intensity. They prepared themselves to hit Solomon with their own power to try and knock him out without seriously hurting him.

Closer and closer Solomon came. The glow of the three colours merged into one, intensifying more and more as Solomon got closer.

"GIVE ME YOUR BEST SHOT, BUGS!" the Bad shouted.

"Are you ready?" Zeal asked.

"Ready as I'll ever be," Caitlin answered.

"Now or never," Balamore said.

Zeal counted down.

"Three. Two." the glow around the three faeries intensified.

"One."

As Zeal reached the last number a bolt of green, gold and sky blue light shot from their bodies.

The stream of colours flew through the wood and a rushing sound followed.

The Bad stood its ground as the light hit and surrounded Solomon's body. A shock wave flew in all directions and the three faeries kept on pushing the light. The colours were flowing faster and faster from their tiny bodies.

The light pulsated and throbbed. More and more the three faeries pushed their energy.

The Bad started to lose its footing. Solomon's feet started to slide backwards on the soil of the wood, as the energy bolts from the three faeries kept hitting him harder and harder. He was being pushed back.

The three faeries could sense this and with one last surge of energy, the three pushed harder. More and more light rushed from their bodies.

The Bad now stared intensely at the three. Turning red and glowing, rage travelled though its eyes. It was surprised by their strength.

Focusing hard, the Bad raised Solomon's arms to his chest and with his hands, formed a small shield. It was time to fight back.

A low thundering sound could be heard coming from the Bad. Louder and louder the noise became. It was like Solomon was gritting his teeth and growling for strength.

Caitlin feeling the Bad fighting back, said, "We can't keep this up."

"One...More...Push!" Zeal urged, and the three of them did.

As they did, a voice screamed through the wood at them. It was the Bad.

"NOOOOOOOOO!"

A booming sound echoed through the wood. Silence followed then an intense explosion.

Caitlin, Zeal, Balamore and Solomon were thrown in opposite directions leaving a crater in the ground. There was smoke and charred wood everywhere.

The three faeries dazed and confused, managed to get back their balance and rejoin each other. Each one was shook up and left feeling tired and drained of energy. After checking each other, they slowly flew over to the crater and looked for Solomon.

A tear ran down Caitlin's face. She thought they had killed him. That tear stopped quickly after they heard from a distance a laugh. Again it was cold and evil.

From the distance, Solomon who was smouldering from the blast and slightly charred was laughing as he was walking towards them.

"You will have to do better than that," the Bad said to the three faeries.

Dejection could be seen on the faces of Zeal, Caitlin and Balamore. They had no more energy and they were tired. They had just about enough energy to keep themselves hovering above the ground.

Solomon was readying himself to throw more fire at them, when a great big shadow came from overhead. The large shadow scooped the three little faeries up into its large claw.

Gerth had flown down after seeing the explosion and knew the three faeries were in trouble.

"Thought you might need a little rest," he said in his deep

bellowing voice.

The three faeries just collapsed and rested, as Gerth flew higher and higher into the sky. The Bad watched as Gerth flew away. He smirked thinking that nothing could stop him.

He had fought a dragon who had blown ice cold air over him. Then, he had taken on three pesky little faeries who were surprisingly powerful. In the end they were no trouble, no match at all.

The Bad smiled to himself, feeling more and more confident that nothing could stop him.

He looked ahead through the maze of trees before him. As he placed one foot in-front of another to start his journey to the village, he was hit by a blue thunderbolt of lightning.

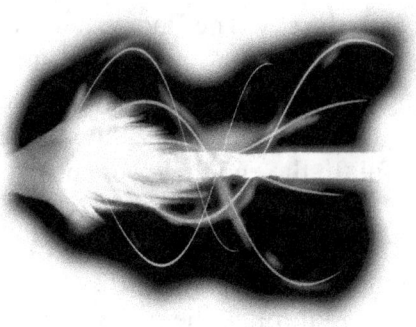

18

– CORNERED –

Five elders connected by a white and blue line of light hovered above the ground. Each looking at Solomon. Each understanding the pain that the little boy must be experiencing while under the influence of the Bad. Each knowing they had to do everything in their powers to stop the evil that was using an innocent young boy.

The five elders. Elder Albizzia Silva Wood. Elder Ignis Succendo Fire. Elder Storm Marsh Fons Water. Elder Fundo Lamnia Metal and Elder Orbis Terrarum Earth.

The five elders of nature, also known as the Elders of life's Elements.

The elders looked on, unmoved by the enormity of the situation or of the power the Bad had at its fingertips. Each elder lowered their hands and looked at what they had done.

The Bad ripped itself from a tree it had been embedded into from the force of the lightning strike. It had left a large rough imprint of Solomon's body on the tree.

The Bad checked its new body and found that it was

miraculously unhurt.

"My powers are getting stronger," it whispered.

The Bad looked ahead seeing the five meddling faeries just floating on thin air. The Bad screamed.

The noise was so loud, that it shook the very branches of every tree in the area and thousands of leaves floated to the ground. The Bad raised it hands, and quickly two large stones next to it were lifted into the air and thrown at the faeries. The stones travelled so fast that it was too late for the five faeries to move, instead they stayed where they were.

The two stones exploded just centimetres away from the faeries. Stone fragments of all sizes shot in all directions. After the rain of stone had quietened down the five faeries were still floating, unmoved by what had happened. They had no marks or injuries.

"I'LL GET YOU!" the Bad shouted.

The five faeries allowed a small smile to appear on their faces. Each one darted in a different direction leaving only a small trail of light as they moved at lightning speed.

They all zigzagged around the Bad. Different intensities of light whipped around Solomon's head. A whizzing sound could be heard and Solomon's face disappeared as the faeries travelled faster and faster. Their light acting like a shield around him. Then a thundering sound came from nowhere.

The ground started to shake and trees started to move. Roots of trees burst through the ground. It was like an earthquake.

The five faeries flew away and after gaining its footing, the Bad saw what made the thunderous noise.

Ten tall oakmen were standing in a line waiting to do battle. Their leader, Autumn Brown Leaf stepped forward.

Thrusting out his huge thick trunk arms, a dozen strands of thin roots shot out from what could be called his fingers, encircling and entangling the Bad where it stood. To one side of Autumn Brown Leaf, were a few oakmen who were carrying Dave, Sarah, Winnie and her friends.

The Bad struggled, being ensnared tightly by the roots. Autumn Brown Leaf lowered his arms and the roots broke away from his fingers. The entrapped Bad was held tight and it looked like he was secure.

The Bad stopped struggling and looked carefully at all who were standing. An evil glimmer in Solomon's eyes could be seen and the oakmen knew something was about to happen.

Solomon's body seemed to shrink only a little. Then from within the snake encircled web of roots, Solomon lowered himself so that he disappeared.

A cloud of soil blew up where he was standing. A few seconds later as the cloud of soil disappeared, Solomon was gone.

With no more than four gigantic strides, Autumn Brown Leaf reached the point where he had ensnared Solomon. He looked at the circle of roots and saw a hole in the ground. With a vibration in the ground, a flash of red light erupted from the hole. A trail of soil on the surface of the ground could be seen, being created like a giant mole was doing the digging.

The trail shot past Autumn Brown Leaf. With split second thinking, Autumn Brown Leaf lunged at the trail of soil with his huge tree trunk feet, trying to stop the tunnelling. The Bad was too quick.

Autumn Brown Leaf faced everyone and shouted, "HE'S GONE UNDERGROUND!"

The other oakmen jumped up into the air, each one landing just short of the oncoming trail of soil. As each oakman landed it dug its huge oak feet into the ground. The fast moving trail suddenly veered to the side going around the oakman and back on its path.

On towards the village the Bad headed, as it left the oakmen who were giving chase. It had no more than a mile to go.

A short while after the confrontation with the oakmen, the Bad was out of the ground and standing on the outskirts of the wood looking out at the village.

Still chasing Solomon, Autumn Brown Leaf looked up at the sky to the dragons and shouted, "DO YOUR BEST!"

Facing his oakmen, Autumn Brown Leaf called up on them to head for the circle, while he would go to the village. The oakman who were carrying Dave and Sarah walked forward and gave them to Autumn Brown Leaf. Then the nine remaining oakmen left for the circle.

"Master Dave and Lady Sarah. If the dragons fail, then you will be our only hope." Dave and Sarah knew what they had to do.

The three of them walked to the village to try to stop Solomon and the Bad.

19

- FIGHT FOR THE VILLAGE -

The village was as always in a state of tranquillity. A cool breeze blew through the village, and overhead a blue sky and the occasional white cloud passed by. In the gardens of homes flowers were in full bloom, stretching their tiny bodies to get the most of the sunshine. Life in the village was blissful for those who lived there.

A few old timers were fishing in the local stream. A number of neighbours were trimming their growing ivy, that had attached itself to the sides and fronts of their cottage homes. On a nearby field, an elderly couple had decided to practice a bit of landscape painting before enrolling on Sarah's painting course.

The elderly couple sitting down, were just finishing up on the blue sky when, as they looked up they saw ahead of them some black patches coming towards them.

"Edith," the woman's husband Cecil called out.

"What is it dear?" Edith answered.

"Do you see some rain clouds coming?"

Edith looked up and saw five black spots approaching rather fast.

"Too fast for rain clouds Cecil. Maybe a flock of black birds?"

Cecil looked at his wife and casually lifted up his eyes as if saying, *"What do you know."*

He looked harder squinting his eyes. As he looked the black spots were getting closer, bigger and started to take shape.

"I...I...I..." was all he could say before being interrupted.

"Stop stuttering dear," Edith said without taking her eyes off the canvas of blue sky she was painting, "You know how it affects your face. You look like something from a horror film."

Cecil stood up and took off his flap cap. With his eyes wide open he couldn't believe what he was seeing. Looking up and holding out his arm with a finger pointing up, he shouted, "DRAGONS!"

Edith looked up. Low and behold, she too saw one, two, three... Five large beasts each wing as long as three double decker buses. They were getting closer.

She stood up and screamed, nearly fainting. Cecil quickly caught her in his arms. His grip was weak and Edith fell to the ground with a loud thud.

As the dragons got closer, Cecil threw himself to the ground as the five massive bodies swooped down close and passed the elderly couple. As the dragons past, Cecil thought he could hear the dragons shout something like, "DANGER!"

It only took a few more seconds for more people to see the fast moving shapes fly over the village. Immediately, the panic stricken villagers were running and screaming.

Those who were cleaning windows fell off their ladders. Some riding bicycles crashed into hedgerows and some fell into the stream. The old timers who were fishing seemed oblivious to why everyone was shouting and screaming.

"Do you mind. I'm trying to catch some fish," one of them shouted without looking round.

A second or two later, an explosion of water erupted and

engulfed the boat and fishermen as the dragons flew past.

The dragons had succeeded in doing what was necessary, which wasn't difficult. They had created a panic that would get the villagers out of the village and far away. This was for the villagers own safety.

The dragons kept on flying up and then scooping down, only missing running scared villagers by a few feet. The dragons were loving it. They thought it was fun, but knew of the importance of their actions.

From nowhere, as if they were invisible, other mythical creatures emerged to add havoc to the situation. Boggarts, goblins, and derricks suddenly appeared.

"WOW!" one of the dragons shouted, "Do you see that?"

One of the goblins had herded up some people and had forced them into a bicycle rental shop. Some of the frantic people just grabbed what they could and rode off down the road, away from the carnage behind them.

The goblin laughed as the people rode away. As with the other creatures, it set about trying to save people as well as giving them a really good scare.

Joining the goblins were earthly creatures such as, otters, foxes, badgers, ravens, crows, eagles and falcons.

From nowhere, thousands of mice turned up. Seeing the mice the frantic villagers seemed to run even faster.

The plan to panic the villagers seemed to be working and hopefully they would all quickly leave the village safely.

For about 20 minutes the badgers, foxes and otters darted and scurried around people. The crows, ravens, eagles and falcons swooped down screeching at the people. The mice jumped and climbed onto people's shoulders and squeaked at them, sending the unfortunate person they landed on into a frenzy. Everywhere a villager turned there would be something wanting to nip or dive at them.

The Bad arrived at the edge of the wood.

It saw the havoc and knew what was happening.

The dragons, boggarts, goblins and derricks, as well as all the other animals and creatures were trying to scare the good people of Birchover village away.

Anger flared inside the Bad and it threw its anger on the first dragon it saw.

A bolt of energy hit the belly of a dragon, knocking it off balance for a short time. The blast got everything and everyone's attention. All eyes looked at the edge of the wood where a little boy was standing.

The dragons growled as they spun around and faced the Bad. There were people to protect and Gerth had to let the people know. With the other four dragons ordered to slow the Bad down, Gerth flew down to the village and landed on one of the roads near the village stream. With other mythical creatures around, the panic stricken people stood still out of fear.

Gerth spoke, "People of this village. Please do not be afraid."

As soon as Gerth spoke, his voice, the words he spoke seemed to have a calming effect on the people of the village. Everyone stopped running and looked at Gerth. He gently flapped his huge wings, while the other four dragons circled around overhead. With his long neck and massive head, he looked at the people with compassion.

"My name is Gerth. As you can see, I am a dragon. A Golden Dragon."

There were a few sighs coming from some of the villagers, but the fear they had was quickly disappearing. Gerth continued.

"I, my fellow dragons as well as the other creatures that you have met in a very unconventional way, are here to help and protect you. I sincerely apologise for the scare that we have caused you. We don't have much time. Simply put, you are all in danger."

An elderly man stepped forward and came very close to Gerth.

Gerth looked down at the him with caring eyes and waited for the man to speak.

"Hel... Hello," the man said, "I'm George. George C. Weston."

"It is an honour to speak to you, Master George C. Weston. A fine name you have," the friendliness by which Gerth addressed the man, made more people walk forward.

"Why are you here?" one man asked.

"What is happening?" another wanted to know.

Gerth shook his head up and down slightly, with a face that showed he understood the reason for their questions.

He said to everyone, "You are all in danger. This will be difficult to understand or comprehend."

Some of the people were feeling a little unsettled by what was being said, but strangely they felt safe in the presence of Gerth. The other four dragons still flew overhead keeping a careful watch on Solomon.

"To the back of me is a little boy who has been taken over by a force of unspeakable evil. The evil is intent on destroying everything that you love and cherish. I, with other mythical creatures that you have read about in story books, have come back from our own realms to protect you and fight the evil."

The murmurings of so many people got rather loud, until Gerth snorted some cold air from his nostrils, then the noise quieten down.

"You have to trust me when I say that you must all flee from here, so that my fellow dragons and I, can fight what we call the Bad."

George, the villager who introduced himself spoke up.

"The young boy, on the edge of the wood, what can he do? He's just a boy."

Gerth understood the necessity of questions, but time was running out.

"We do not have much time my good friend. You must believe me when I say that something evil and very old has taken over that innocent boy. We are trying all we can to save him and destroy the evil. But, your safety is also important."

Another elderly man spoke up, "If this morning someone had told me that faery tales were true, or I'd see a flying dragon let alone five, I'd laugh in that person's face. But you are here. You are real. As real as the person standing next to me. So, I have to believe what you are saying, no matter how weird or absurd it may seem."

158

The more people thought about it, the more the reality of the situation sunk in. Suddenly and quite unexpectedly, nearly all of the villagers jeered in the direction of the the Bad.

Solomon was still standing at the edge of the wood. The monster inside him ready for a fight.

The Bad watched curiously what was happening.

One of the villagers turned to face Gerth and said, "We may not have the strength or what magic you posses, but this here is our land, our village, our home. Nothing is going to scare us away from here. If you fight, we will fight along side you."

There was a cheer that filled the air and could be heard for miles. Gerth listened to the words and was touched by the lionhearted attitude of the people. He felt deep inside the memories of the old days, when he fought side by side with the King of England a thousand years ago.

"People of Birchover Village. I, my dragons and the creatures you see around you, will be proud to have you fight by our sides. We will stand together. We will stand strong."

Gerth instructed everyone, to get what weapons they could find and to stand behind him and the other mythical creatures that were readying for battle.

People picked up rakes, sticks, cricket bats, nets and anything else they could carry. It was like times of old and Gerth, as well as all the other creatures felt proud.

The mothers and women of the village had taken refuge with the children in the local church, while the men stood behind Gerth.

The fight against the Bad had begun.

The Bad stood there on the edge of the wood, looking down at the villagers who had sided with the creatures of faery tales. It smirked at them and said in a loud thunderous voice, "People of Birchover Village. Petty fools. Standing behind an overgrown house pet will not save you. I will show you no mercy. Your lives will end today."

Solomon raised his arms, opened his hands and from his palms hundreds of ice spears shot out at a ferocious speed heading for the villagers. Everyone from the village gasped in horror, but

159

the dragons were also quick.

The four dragons that were in the air, quickly dropped from the sky and landed, digging their massive claws into the ground for extra grip. All the dragons, including Gerth opened their huge wings to protect all the villagers from the deadly shower of ice spears. Every single spear hit the dragons, but with their tough skin none of the ice spears caused any damage. The ice just shattered apart after hitting the dragons.

Once the rain of ice stopped, the dragons folded back their wings. Immediately four of the dragons leapt into the air and spat intense fireballs at Solomon. The fireballs exploded in-front, behind and at the sides of the boy, leaving huge craters in the ground.

Solomon laughed and another four fireballs came hurtling at him. Long tails of fire streaked through the sky. Heat blazing with such intensity, the fireballs were as hot as volcanic lava. The dragons had found their target perfectly. This time all four fireballs were heading straight at Solomon.

A crowd of creatures had gathered around the Nine Ladies Stone Circle, with the elders of the faeries taking charge and calming down everything and everyone there. Elder Perennial Swallowtail glowed as he entered the circle. He hovered and placed himself into a trance. He closed his eyes and the colour of his aura covered him. Nothing could see him except for his glowing light.

A few minutes passed by and his colour died down. Opening his eyes, Elder Perennial Swallowtail addressed the crowd.

"Patience, my friends. Patience. The dragons and our other friends have met with the villagers. As of now, the dragons are battling the Bad and protecting the village."

There was a murmur among the gathering, suggesting that all were nervous about the situation. There was nothing they could do but wait. And wait they did.

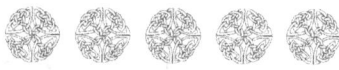

The Bad placed Solomon's arms in a cross shape, in-front of itself as the fireballs came blazing towards it. With only a few feet left before they would devour him, all four fireballs exploded showering everything around him. Like liquid, the fire poured out from the sky leaving Solomon unscathed.

Solomon laughed and everyone heard the evil, diabolical laughter of the Bad. It sent a cold feeling through everyone's body.

Solomon looked up at one of the dragons flying away. He raised his two arms. Blue and white energy bolts encircled them, starting from his shoulders and gaining speed as they reached his open hands. He targeted huge amounts of energy at the passing dragon. Electricity bolts shot out of every finger.

The lightning strike hit the dragon on one of its wings.

A roar of pain left the mouth of the dragon and it started to plummet to earth. The huge animal spiralled out of control, leaving a trail of black smoke behind it.

Everyone heard the loud crash and an explosion of trees, as the poor dragon hit the wood sending up massive mounds of soil and wood into the air. A few moments passed and there was no sign, no noise to indicate the dragon had survived. Everyone and everything looked in the direction of the fallen dragon.

Gerth looked away as a tear trickled down the side of his face. He looked at the Bad who was still standing and grinning from ear to ear.

"I WILL TAKE MY REVENGE!" Gerth yelled.

He raised his huge wings and with one giant flap, he was in the air ready to do battle.

A group of young men ran towards the crash site of the fallen dragon, to see if there was anything they could do. The other three dragons were still in the air. They turned their attention to the Bad and could feel rage taking over.

In quick succession, the dragons blew fire and ice at the

same time. They were replying with anger, rather than tactics to defeat or at least slow the Bad down. It had an effect but it was only temporary.

As soon as the effects of the fire and ice wore off, Solomon started to walk towards the village with only one intention, total destruction of everything there.

Explosions rocketed the land. Fireballs exploded all around the Bad. The ground cracked underneath his feet from the shear coldness of the ice breath coming from the dragons.

The Bad sent streams and streams of lightning, high energy bolts and more ice spears at the dragons, but even when these hit the dragons they fought on, never letting up.

They would only stop fighting when every one of them was dead.

Meanwhile, the people of the village were throwing stones and anything else they could get their hands on at Solomon. Their actions proved worthless, as Solomon just knocked everyone to the ground by slamming his palms together, generating a loud sound wave, which hit everyone standing.

His eyes flashed red then beams of red light cut into the ground, just in-front of everyone. It looked like there was no hope. The Bad seemed invincible.

People started to believe that nothing could stop it.

The villagers started to run in all directions, and the dragons were flying on the last of their strength.

A little hope appeared.

Solomon was nearly at the edge of the village. The field he was walking down was ablaze, and people full of desperation were still throwing anything they could get their hands on at him. Then came a crashing noise from the wood that earned the Bad's attention.

The thing that was making the noise showed itself. Autumn Brown Leaf.

The tall ancient and majestic tree stood on the edge of the wood roaring at the Bad. Autumn Brown Leaf looked at what had occurred. He was still carrying Dave and Sarah in his arms.

Everyone from the village saw the tall tree man.

162

The oakman was standing tall and ready for battle. Autumn Brown Leaf was posed for whatever was necessary to end this war.

"COWARD!" Autumn Brown Leaf roared at the Bad.

"FACE ME. DO NOT RUN AWAY, AGAIN!"

The Bad spun round, not liking what it heard from a tree. It thought that the tree was nothing. It would dispose of that menacing walking talking piece of wood, and every other tree once he had finished with the village. Solomon turned back to face the village and continued to walk towards the people.

Without hesitation, Sarah jumped out of Autumn Brown Leaf's arms and walked forward.

"Solomon!" Sarah shouted, "SOLOMON!" her voice was carried by the passing breeze.

She shouted again, "SOLOMON!"

Then the Bad heard Sarah shouting.

It turned around and saw Sarah standing there with her arms held out.

"Solomon! It's me. Your mother. Can you hear me? Please come back."

The Bad just stood there and did nothing. Then Dave jumped down from Autumn Brown Leaf's arms.

"Solomon! This is your father. Listen to your mother. Come here, now!"

Hearing his father's voice was like a jolt of electricity to Solomon.

The Bad started to twitch and shake. The shaking got physically violent. Solomon hit the ground and screamed. He started to pound the ground with clenched fists.

"MUUUUUMMMMMM! DAAAAADDDDDD!"

Dave and Sarah both shouted at the same time, "SOLOMON! COME HERE, NOW! STAND UP AND WALK TOWARDS US!"

He got up tears running down his cheeks. Just as Dave and Sarah thought they had reached out to Solomon, a smile appeared on their son's face.

"You think you can have Solomon, your son! Your precious little son! He's mine. ALL MINE!" the Bad screamed out.

"I'll deal with these meddling villagers later. I want you two."

Pointing at his parents he started walking towards them.

"Quick. Back in my arms," Autumn Brown Leaf ordered.

Sarah and Dave quickly climbed back onto Autumn Brown Leaf. Once they were safely on him, Autumn Brown Leaf turned and went back into the wood.

20

- THE FINAL FIGHT -

Autumn Brown Leaf walked as fast as he could, carrying both Dave and Sarah in his huge wooden arms, but held them gently as if they were just small children.

"Where are you going? Where are you taking us?" Dave asked.

"Don't worry. Just keep calling out to Solomon. He will follow us now," Autumn Brown Leaf said.

Dave and Sarah did just that. They kept calling out to their son, which made the Bad more furious.

It kept on following the sounds of Solomon's parents calling out. The Bad was acting like a fish caught on a fishing line, unable to get away. It had to follow the voices. It felt compelled to do so. It was also obsessed with destroying the walking trees.

Occasionally, the Bad would throw anything it could at what it thought was Autumn Brown Leaf. The tree was far away, so whatever the Bad threw at him would just hit other trees in the wood. Even though the trees protected Dave, Sarah and Autumn Brown Leaf, it made the oakman very angry that trees were taking the brunt of the attack.

"The trees have done nothing to him," Autumn Brown Leaf

sounded distressed, but the old tree man kept walking through the wood. Occasionally feeling he wanted to turn back and face the monster that was pursuing them. He knew he couldn't. It was essential that the Bad kept on following the three of them. The chase was relentless.

The one thing that the Bad didn't notice was that he was heading towards higher ground. It didn't notice because it didn't care. The Bad had one thing on its mind, it wanted to destroy the tree and Solomon's parents.

"Nearly there," Autumn Brown Leaf said to Dave and Sarah.

They continued making their way through the wood, still hearing the Bad making loud noises and crashing sounds that seemed to be falling trees. A few minutes later, Autumn Brown Leaf with one last giant stretch of his legs broke through a line of trees.

Stepping into a clear opening, Autumn Brown Leaf, Sarah and Dave were greeted by all the faeries. Especially by the elders led by Elder Swallowtail.

"Finally you are here," Elder Swallowtail said.

Directing all his words to everyone, he said, "Now everyone, disappear."

With lightning speed, everything hid among the trees and the whole area was as quiet as a grave yard. Autumn Brown Leaf walked to the far side of the stone circle and waited for the Bad.

The sound of crashing trees coming from the wood was getting louder and louder.

Just before the Bad smashed through to the clearing, Autumn Brown Leaf said to Dave and Sarah, "If everything goes well, little Solomon will be saved and back in your arms before the setting sun."

They were words both Dave and Sarah needed to hear, for a second later the Bad smashed through a line of trees and stood on the other side of the stone circle.

It looked at Autumn Brown Leaf with hungry, menacing glowing red eyes. Its eyes said only one thing, destruction! It had come all this way from the village and wasn't going back until

Dave, Sarah and Autumn Brown Leaf were gone from this place forever.

Solomon stood panting and looking a little drained of energy. The four dragons who it had battled earlier were flying high in the sky, circling the wood like eagles protecting their nest.

The time had come for Dave, Sarah and Autumn Brown Leaf to face the Bad. It was time to try and save Solomon. To save him from the influence he was under. This was not going to be easy!

Immediately, the Bad raised Solomon's arms and sent a shower of stones and rocks hurtling at Autumn Brown Leaf.

With split second timing, Autumn Brown Leaf raised up his arms and a curtain of soil flew up from the ground. Like an impenetrable shield, it protected Dave and Sarah from the stones and rocks that pummelled the curtain of soil.

As each stone hit the soil it lost its energy and just fell to the ground.

The Bad roared at the tree and the ancient tree quickly took charge of the situation.

With a flick of a wooden finger, a tornado erupted all around Solomon. The walls of the tornado were made up of twigs, branches, leaves, stones and soil. It was all kept together by a strong current of air.

Autumn Brown Leaf kept twirling his wooden finger and as he did, the tornado became stronger and stronger.

Sarah and Dave were feeling the strain of seeing their son being used in this way, but they knew deep down that it was for the best. It was the only way. They had placed their faith and trust in the hands of the mythical creature's.

The tornado kept on spinning and gathering speed. The faster it spun, the more twigs, leaves and soil it whipped up into its funnel. Increasing in size, strength and ferociousness.

Inside, Solomon closed his eyes and concentrated. With flashes of white and blue light, and a sound of crackling thunder coming from inside the tornado, Solomon threw out his arms in opposite directions. The tornado ripped apart.

Branches, soil and everything else that made up the walls of

167

the tornado, fell to the ground.

All the trees in the area that had been batted by the tornado settled down. The whole area was quiet for a brief moment.

Dave and Sarah could now see how angry the Bad was.

The Bad had conjured up so much energy and power to break free from the tornado, that hot steam could be seen coming from Solomon's body. The very ground Solomon was standing on was smoking, cooked to a crisp.

"What do we do? What do we do?" Sarah said anxiously.

Autumn Brown Leaf said to her, "Have faith. Call out to him."

Sarah didn't have to be told twice. She felt Autumn Brown Leaf's grip loosen.

She jumped down, and on the edge of the stone circle she called out her son's name, "Solomon. Solomon. Listen to me."

Solomon seemed not to listen to his mother, so she called out to him again using a stronger voice.

"Solomon! Listen to me. It's your mother."

Nothing seemed to work. Sarah was feeling panicky and didn't know what to do. She looked up at the sky to search for answers. As she was feeling desperate and hopeless, the answer came to her.

A dragon was flying over head, ready to snatch Sarah and Dave to safety if the situation became worse. But instead of seeing a dragon, Sarah saw Solomon's best friend instead. She took in a deep breath and changed her face to one that showed anger. She then looked directly at her son pointing a finger at him.

She said, "Solomon! If you do not listen to your mother, then you will not see Rupert ever again. Do you hear me!"

The eyes and expression of the Bad changed. Sarah recognised Solomon.

"MUM!" Solomon cried out, "HELP ME!"

Everyone who was there knew that was Solomon calling out to his mother.

Sarah was ready to run to him, but couldn't. Solomon would have to come to her.

"Solomon," Sarah said, "Come to me. Come now and I will

save you. We can be together in each other's arms."

Tears rolled down both their faces. Solomon listened and Sarah could see her son fighting the Bad for control of his body.

"COME ON, Solomon!" Sarah screamed, "Rupert is waiting. Your father and I are waiting."

Just then, Solomon moved forward and into the Nine Ladies Stone Circle.

As Solomon walked slowly forward, he called out to his mother and Sarah called out to him.

"You can do it, Solomon. I'm here. I will protect you."

Without warning, Solomon's face changed and a sinister smile appeared.

"And who will protect you?" came the voice.

The Bad had taken back Solomon's body.

The energy and emotion that Sarah had conjured up, just flowed away in a pool of hopelessness.

The Bad moved forward faster into the circle. It was now in the centre.

The Bad stopped.

From behind Autumn Brown Leaf came the five elders of Elements, accompanied by Elder Perennial Swallowtail, Elder Dandelion Green Leaf and two other elders of the faery order.

"What are you doing?" the Bad asked with a curious tone.

It seemed stuck to the spot but still standing in the centre of the circle.

"What needs to be done," Elder Swallowtail said.

Autumn Brown Leaf was now standing with his brethren. Seeing the Bad standing in the centre of the circle, he clicked two large fingers.

The sound shook the trees surrounding the area.

Immediately nine long roots shot out from under each of the nine stones out across the circle, wrapping themselves around Solomon's legs. The Bad looked and laughed.

"You think you can bind me up one more time?" it said, "I don't think so."

The Bad tried to kick out a leg but couldn't. It tried to kick again but found that both legs were held so tight, it couldn't move.

It tried again but still no movement.

"Wh...What is this?" it cried out.

All nine elders had positioned themselves around the circle. Each elder standing on one of the stones that made up the stone circle.

Nine elders for nine stones.

"You...You can't do this. I...I won't let you. Solomon will die if you try anything."

The Bad tried all sorts of threats until Elder Perennial Swallowtail spoke.

"ENOUGH! You can threaten and you can struggle, but now that you are inside the Nine Ladies Stone Circle, your powers lie dormant."

The Bad threw out a hand and nothing happened. It tried it again and still nothing. Its powers were gone.

"I...I don't believe this. This can't be," the Bad screamed out, "How can this be! HOW CAN THIS BE!"

Elder Swallowtail spoke again, "Where you are standing is a sacred place. Not just for the mythical creatures that dwell in stories, but it is sacred to the place we live."

His voice was strong speaking to the Bad and not to Solomon.

"Our earth, the earth of human kind and for every living creature. This is a place that cannot be touched or tainted by evil. Your powers have no place here. As long as you remain in the circle you will be powerless."

The Bad struggled more and more but it was hopeless.

"So, you are going to try and keep me here for all eternity?" It screamed out again.

With a stern face, Elder Swallowtail looked at the Bad.

"No. You need to be stopped. You are a danger to everyone and everything." he paused, "Sadly, the only option we in the mythical world have is to destroy you. You will be no more."

Elder Swallowtail face changed. His tone of voiced changed and spoke to the monster with a heavy heart.

"When we first met I knew who you were, or in truth what you were. A human. Cassava Oxalic Solari. You were gifted with

170

knowledge of herbs and the arts of healing, but vanity grew in your heart. You wanted more. You wanted the power of life over death, which is a power that YOU can never have."

The Bad tried to pull the roots away with all of its strength when it heard its human name. It was still unable to break them.

"Since your imprisonment, I have tried to think of ways for you to become what you once were. Even to pursue a way of becoming one of us, but alas, there is no spell, no magic, no cure for what you are. You will never change and that is why I cannot help you."

The Bad started to laugh, and as it did all nine elders started to chant words from an ancient time.

"Val tuulo kelvar protec coia. Gerth del auta tuulo naneth kemen auta ee-ah" (*power from nature protect life. Death Strike the horror and take away from mother Earth. Send to the abyss*)

The nine stones started to glow. Each one emitting a beautiful glow of dark blue, which occasionally changed to blood red and then back again to sky blue.

"Val tuulo kelvar protec coia."

The elders repeated the chant and it also became louder.

"Gerth del auta tuulo naneth kemen auta ee-ah."

The Bad started to struggle more. As the chant became louder, the more the Bad struggled. Then it happened.

Each elder of each stone, starting with Elder Perennial Swallowtail crossed their arms. As they did, a blue light shot out of Elder Swallowtail. The light joined the elder to the left of him, until the light had joined all the elders together forming a blue circle of light. Then, each stone emitted a white glow, which started from the base of each stone and covered each elder. When each elder was covered, the glow formed a larger circle.

Everyone could see all the elders were still attached by the blue circle of light.

The white glowing light throbbed, then turned to a deep red and orange colour. It looked like all the elders were on fire. Just then a blue and green light appeared, wrapping itself around the red and orange light like a snake. It constantly moved round and through each faery.

The chanting stopped and all that could be heard was a humming noise.

"No! No! NO!" the Bad shouted out.

"It has to be," came the words from each elder.

All spoke as one, "We are sorry."

The humming noise stopped. Silence surrounded everything. Then a beam of light burst from each of the nine elders.

Each beam hit the Bad at the same time. For a few seconds, everyone surrounding the circle had to look away as the white beams were so bright. As everyone's eyes adjusted to the light, they saw what was happening.

First, a scream broke the silence. It was the scream of the Bad, but then a little boy's scream could be heard getting louder and louder.

The beams of light intensified.

With every passing second the beams throbbed. Pulses of energy shot out of each elder and hit the Bad where it stood. As each energy pulse hit the Bad, the next would hit harder and faster. This continued until the pulses were travelling so fast, it just looked like one continuous pulse of light.

Then everything stopped dead.

The beams of light stopped. The glow of the stones died down. And the whole wood turned from day to night then back to day.

All that remained was the Bad. It was glowing covered by a thin veil of white light.

Dave now standing by his wife shouted, "LOOK!" and pointed at what he saw.

The small stone that was given to Dave and Solomon by Caitlin was still in the pocket of Solomon's trousers.

It started to glow a dull yellow. The colour seemed to reach a pitch then it covered and replaced the veil of white light that covered the Bad. The light started to throb gaining speed and energy.

Everything and everyone could see the Bad saying something, but its voice was drummed out by the most amazing thing happening.

The throbbing yellow light started to move up and away from Solomon.

All eyes were on this yellow light.

As it started to drift upwards and away from Solomon, everyone and everything saw what was in the centre of it. The Bad.

The black slime wriggled, but was powerless to break the light. This light prison drifted up taking the black slime, the Bad with it, until it was a safe distance from Solomon, then it stopped and hovered.

All could see the black thing struggling to break free, but its prison was unbreakable for the short time it had left.

There was one last gasp of a struggle from the black slime, then the yellow light seemed to suck in air. The captured beast started to shake violently.

For the last few seconds everything stood waiting for the end to come.

There was a pause. Seconds seemed like hours. The light collapsed onto the beast, covering it completely.

The Bad and the prison that held it exploded, sending a million yellow star like objects in all directions.

Everyone saw the stars slowly fall back down to earth. The starry objects hit everything and everyone, passing through until they hit the ground and disappeared.

The light from the stone circle faded away and all the elders floated down and stood on each stone.

Elder Perennial Swallowtail flew to the centre of the circle where Solomon was. After inspecting the worn out boy, the elder made an announcement.

"The Bad is no more. Solomon is alive and well. Safe once more."

Every living thing shouted and screamed for joy.

Right away, Dave and Sarah ran towards Solomon who had fallen to his knees. As they got to him, all the cheerful noise died down.

Dave picked him up.

Sarah said to him in a gentle voice, "Solomon. Solomon.

Can you hear me?"

Solomon raised his head, smiled and simply said in a croaky voice, "I love you."

The whole wood erupted in a great cheer and laughter. Solomon was alive and well and the Bad was finely destroyed, forever.

21

- RETURN TO VILLAGE LIFE -

I t took some time for normality to return to Birchover Village.

After Solomon was taken back to his parents home, the faeries got to work to help him recover from his nightmare ordeal. Feeding him ancient herbs and of course, telling him stories of myths, magic and folklore.

Also, they helped to educate the villagers about the wood and that all the stories they had read when they were young, were all true.

For the dragon that crashed landed in the wood, he was being looked after everyday by the local children. They had called him Black Tip. After the lightning bolt and his crash landing, he had gotten a permanent burn mark at the end of one of his wing tips. Never had Black Tip ever been treated with such kindness. He loved having the children around.

Slowly, all the woodland creatures such as the badgers, foxes, mice, and all the birds, as well as the mythical creatures of the wood disappeared back to where they came from. Leaving only the oakmen, dragons and faeries left to say their goodbyes.

The whole village had turned out to say, "Thank you," to

the dragons, oakmen and faeries.

In a thousand years this had not happened, and it brought back good memories for every mythical creature.

Autumn Brown Leaf was first to speak, "I am a tree of few words so this will be short," he started to say.

"I am pleased to see the wood that looks upon the village is thriving and plentiful with wildlife. Remember, that all trees are alive and must be treated as you would treat each other. Thank you."

Autumn Brown Leaf and the other trees all smiled, as the villagers clapped and cheered. It was now time for Gerth to speak.

"Villagers of Birchover. Be proud of what you have accomplished," a beast of great size spoke with a gentle and soothing voice.

"You have believed the unimaginable. Seen the incredible. You fought the impossible. You stood by our sides as allies and friends. You will never be forgotten. Tell your children, and let your children tell their children what happened in Birchover village. Never let that magic die."

Gerth took a deep breath and said, "I and the realm of dragons will always be your protectors."

The whole crowd felt a feeling similar to when you see a long lost loved one, and the feeling works it way up from your stomach to the tears that roll down your face.

All the dragons lifted gently into the sky and when they formed a line, they turned and swept down heading for the villagers. With perfect timing all the dragons tilted a wing, and they flew across the heads of all villagers only missing them by a few feet.

The people watched in amazement as the dragons lifted themselves higher into the sky.

They heard a majestic voice shout out, "Thank you."

Everyone looking at the dragons saw the wonderful creatures slowly disappear, the same way they appeared. The sky became silent.

Everyone looked down and then saw the oakmen walk away. As they reached the edge of the wood they too disappeared, their spirits mingled with the trees of Birchover wood.

A sudden breeze filled the area and everyone from the village quietly said to the wood, "Thank you. We will miss you."

All that was left, was a large gathering of faeries floating in a magical gathering of spectacular colour. The oldest and most respected of the faeries came closer to the villagers. Elder Swallowtail spoke to them, "Friends. You have all born witness to magic that has not been seen for a thousand years, and probably will never been seen again," the crowd listened intently.

"There is one thing that I must say to you, before my kind go back into the wood where we belong," everyone went quiet.

"If you come looking for us in the wood, you will not find us. If you tell the world about us, they will not find us or believe you. We will only show ourselves when there is a time of great need, or when there is a lost child in the wood. The time for your world and the world of myths, legends and folklore to live side by side as they once did, that time is not yet and may never be."

His face said he wished it was, as his mind was thinking about a certain event hundreds of years ago. It made the faeries and the creatures of folklore hide from humans altogether.

Yes, humans were leaning towards science for answers and guidance, but the mythical creatures could of co-existed with them.

"Whether that time will ever come again is difficult to see, but deep down I believe it will come, only because of some catalytic event in the future."

Elder Perennial Swallowtail looked at a couple at the front of the crowd.

Dave and Sarah were standing together with their arms around Solomon. Solomon was feeling great and wonderful. The faeries also helped cure his breathing problem.

Elder Swallowtail motioned them to step forward and they did. He then spoke to each one of them in their ears, whispering to them, then he backed away and addressed the crowd again.

"Do not pester Dave, Sarah and little Solomon. Please, do hold dear what you have done. We are all friends and when the time is right, we will show ourselves again. Be proud you helped each other and be at peace."

Elder Perennial Swallowtail flew away into the wood and as he did, the gathering of faeries in what seemed like a light show of colours, did the same. After a few moments, the people saw the wood of Birchover light up in a spectrum of colours. Moments later, the light show disappeared.

The wood was now like it had always been. Quiet but full of life.

Everyone then departed.

Somehow, no-one spoke about what they had witnessed. It was like it never happened, except for Dave, Sarah, Solomon, Winnie and her friends.

As everyone walked away, Solomon, Dave and Sarah knew it was time for them to go back to their house.

Winnie came to them and said, "Wonderful. Magical. Bedtime stories that came to life."

As Dave and Sarah thought about it they knew she was right. Winnie said she would see them later in the week, then off she went saying goodbye to them.

Dave, Sarah and Solomon headed back to their house. When they entered it, Solomon ran upstairs and there on his bed was Rupert. He came running downstairs with Rupert in his arms and said, "Mum. Dad. I love you."

Months passed and no one talked about what happened with the mythical creatures. The battle against the Bad. The Nine Ladies Stone Circle and saving of Solomon. Nothing was mentioned.

Dave, Sarah and Solomon knew this would happen. It was one of the things they were told about when Elder Perennial Swallowtail whispered in their ears. But there was more to his message.

"In time," he told them, Solomon, Dave and Sarah would be permitted, as well as Winnie and her group of friends to visit the wood and mingle with the faeries any time they wanted to. They would have a privilege that only a king and a few chosen ones had once had. Any time that any of them found themselves deep in the wood, all they had to do was call out a name of a faery and they would not be alone again.

Elder Perennial Swallowtail finished off by saying, "We are all family."

22

-FOREVER FRIENDS
&
FAMILY-

Solomon couldn't stop entering the wood whenever he
was at home. He would rush into the house after coming home
from school, change his clothes, grab a drink and, "See later Mum.
Dad," off he would go straight into the wood to meet his best
friends.

If he had been on a long journey to visit family, again he
would rush in and off into the wood. Dave and Sarah just couldn't
stop him from visiting his very special friends. They never worried
and always when daylight was fading, Dave and Sarah knew the
faeries would get Solomon home before it got too late.

This happened practically every day and the faeries never
got tired of seeing Solomon. It only made the magic between faery
and human stronger.

Occasionally, Solomon's parents would also go with him. It
energised them, invigorated them. They would never get use to the

idea of mythical creatures living at the end of their garden. It was a happy time for everyone.

Many times they would also visit Winnie, either at her home or in the wood, as well as the rest of the small group, that had the privilege of know about the wondrous creatures and what happened just a few months ago.

Winnie always made sure she had a bag of goodies she took with her into the wood, so that any creature would be fed if it was feeling a little peckish.

One afternoon before Solomon could rush off into the wood, Sarah asked him and Dave to sit down, as she had something to tell them.

"Oh Mum!" Solomon moaned.

"Don't worry, you'll forgive me for this little interruption. But, it is important," Sarah said.

Dave looked a little confused.

"Sarah," he said, "Are you feeling okay?"

"Wonderful," she answered, "I need to tell you something."

Both Dave and Solomon looked at Sarah and waited for what she had to say.

The pause seemed like hours for Solomon, "Mum, hurry up."

"Okay, okay," Sarah said, with a big smile that showed she couldn't hold her delight any longer, "I would like to say that it is official. I have checked. Dave, Solomon. I'm pregnant!"

Dave slowly stood up with a look on his face that said, "HOW!" then he rushed forward with a huge smile and hugged Sarah.

For Solomon, he was trying to work the situation out, but his expression was of pure delight.

"Wow!" he yelled, "I'm going to have a brother or sister."

He started to jump into the air.

Dave looked at Sarah, "This is wonderful," and the three of them hugged each other.

Solomon then jumped back and asked, "Can I go now and tell the faeries of the good news?"

Sarah placed her cupped hands under Solomon's chin,

kissed his forehead and said, "Of course you can."

After Sarah let go of her son, Solomon rushed out through the patio doors and into the wood, so he could tell them of the great news.

As soon as he reached the wood, Caitlin sensed Solomon's unusual excitement. She quickly gathered Zeal and Balamore, and the three of them rushed through the wood to meet him.

The three of them soon found Solomon, who was panting from the extra energy he put into running through the wood.

Looking at him, Balamore asked with a laughter in his voice, "Are you still trying to chase baby rabbits again, Solomon."

"I think not," Zeal said, "more like being chased by them."

The three of them laughed and as soon as Solomon got his breath back, he also laughed with them.

Shaking his head from side to side and making a deep swallowing sound he managed to speak.

"N...No, I have some great news."

This delighted the three of them, "Go on," Caitlin said.

Solomon took a deep breath and said, "I'm going to have a brother or a sister."

Caitlin understood straight away and quickly flew to his cheek and kissed him. A few seconds later after Zeal and Balamore understood, they screamed with delight, "That's wonderful!"

After leading Solomon through the wood to the rest of the faeries, it wasn't long before everyone knew about the news. Even the trees of the wood moved to express their feelings of joy. It was a great day for all.

Elder Perennial Swallowtail came over and congratulated Solomon, and told him, "You now have a very important job in your family."

He explained, that his mum and dad would need all the help they can get from him, and when the little one arrives he would not just be a brother, but a protector, a teacher and best friend to the new arrival.

Everything that Elder Swallowtail said, Solomon listened, accepted and understood.

He also explained to Solomon that now that they know, Sup

Sup Rose would do what he could to help his mother and the little one when he or she arrives. In-fact, all the faeries promised to help out.

"It's what we love to do," Caitlin said, "Even more so now that your whole family knows about us. It will be even more special."

Solomon stayed in the wood for a few hours until it was time to go. Caitlin, Zeal, Balamore, Sup Sup Rose and Elder Perennial Swallowtail took Solomon home and visited Dave and Sarah.

There they explained what they would do and it was a pleasure to do so.

Dave and Sarah were moved with joy and thanked them for everything they had done so far. The faeries left feeling happy.

After having a quick bite to eat, Solomon went upstairs had a shower and went to bed dreaming of the new arrival.

Nine months later, Solomon stood in the hospital room where his mother lay, tired and still aching from giving birth a few days before.

Dave stood next to Sarah holding Solomon's two sisters.
Annalisa and Samantha.

- THE BRETHREN -
Chapter One - Darkness

A gathering of faeries had assembled at a location not known by many. The gathering was made up by just three faeries that were different.

They all hid their faces under dark leather cloaks and hoods. Their fingers barely broke through the shadow of their sleeves. They hovered off the floor with no visible signs of legs, but behind each one of these hooded beings were foot prints that each had made.

Their wings flapped slowly not making a sound, and each of the creatures breathing was deep. They gathered within a triangle formation and two were looking at one. The one slightly taller than the other two.

Two of the faeries each held a weapon. A spear.

The shaft of the spears were made of oak wood, and the long spear head was made from a mixture of steal, bronze and silver. From the tip of the spear head the blade spilt into three parts. At the end of each blade was curved to a sharp tip.

The other faery had a sword. The handle or grip, was made of silver and was carved to look like the neck of a dragon, with strands of leather wrapped within the grooves of the neck. The guard was the mouth of a dragon with two long silver whiskers travelling in opposite directions. The dragons mouth held the blade. The blade could not been seen as it was inside its scabbard, which was attached to the back of the faery.

One of the two spoke, "My Lord," his voice was rough sounding and cold.

"If we strike now, we can take full control and you will have total authority over those insects, rather than Swallowtail."

The one with the sword, raised its hand as to stop the one from talking.

"Watch your tongue my faithful servant," a smooth slow controlled voice echoed from the hidden face, "I understand your impatience, but those insects you describe are our brethren. Our brothers. Even if they are ruled by a self-righteous, long in the tooth Elder."

The two with spears gave out a low mumbling chuckling sound.

One of them again spoke. It had the voice of a woman, "We have 10,000 Hellebore warriors waiting to turn the ground red. All waiting for your command."

The one spoke, "Yes we have. Soon my Nightshade spies will report back to me."

He points his fingers to the two with spears.

"Now go. Prepare the Hellebore warriors, and get ready for my command."

The two lowered their heads in submission to the one. They then flew away to prepare the warriors for battle.

The one floated to the ground, bent down and picked up some soil. Analysing the soil the faery said, "We are of this earth, and I will send you back to it Elder Swallowtail."

The creatures eyes glowed a fiery red, then it flew away awaiting for news from its trusted and loyal deadly Nightshade spies.

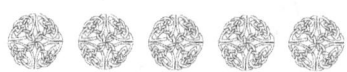

The Nightshade spies had reached there destination. They looked on staring, accessing the situation, always eyeing up the dangers or opportunities of their mission, knowing it was only a matter of a short time before they made their move.

In their minds, those they were spying on, led by the ever peaceful, ever careful Elder Perennial Swallowtail would soon come to an end.

The group looked on from a distance, hidden by leaves from the surrounding woodland, watching the busy faeries exiting and entering a large cave. This small group of seven spies would later report back to their leader with their findings. Everything was reported, nothing was left to chance. Information gathering was of the up most importance.

These seven were not only deadly killers, but were skilled information gatherers.

They were part of a much larger group who had ideas of domination and chaos. To bring to reality all the monsters that showed their eyes in shadows. The growls from behind. The things you see in the corner of your eye, but never see when you turn to look. The presence that can be felt on the back of your neck, but can't be touched. All these scary apparitions, these ghouls of the night and nightmares were to be brought back and used.

The group called themselves "True Faeries." They thought that the present system of ruling from the faery order was weak and always in the shadows of humans. Instead, they thought that they should show themselves to the humans and to make the humans work for them. In their eyes they thought that watching over sleeping children was a waste of time and undeserving.

Their thoughts were, that the protection of the crops should be stopped and farmers should pay for the right of protection. In-fact, humans should be enslaved and the true power of faeries should be shown to the whole world.

This group of faeries had a heart of betrayal, and an evil streak ran through it. Led by their power hungry leader.

The Dark Faeries wanted total domination of the faery order, and if any faery disagreed then that faery would be taken away.

Next, they would plot to enslave the human race.

No mother, father or child would be sparred. If any kingly rule tried to stand up against the Dark Faeries, then the full force of myths, legends and folklore would be unleashed on that kingly rule. Until it succumbed to the Dark Faery order or was completely destroyed.

The spies looked on, and once the entrance was all clear the they carefully entered the cave, quietly almost as if they were invisible.

After entering they immediately mingled with the shadows of the cave, and observed the busy workforce inside. Their orders were to only gather information and under no circumstances must they engage the enemy. This they did, as disobeying the order of their leader would mean imminent death.

The seven spies found good locations, not too close, but close enough to see what was happening. Their own illumination was dark. This happened once they swore allegiance to the darkness. Darkness of shadows was now their ally and protector.

Each one of them observed and could see a flurry of activity, which showed that the chance of being seen was pretty unlikely, so long as they stayed within the shadows of the cave they would be well concealed.

Each spy settled into a crack and observed.

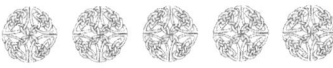

It was like watching a million fireflies dancing to an invisible musical melody. All moving in sync with one another. If one could look closely, then one would notice that these were no fireflies and was no trick of the light inside the magnificent Poole's Cavern.

With a noise of gushing water flowing through the cave, caused by the miraculous filtration process of water flowing through the Derbyshire hills and into the cave. It passed through and out of the cave to the naturally formed rivers, streams and lakes of the surrounding village of Burbage, Buxton.

It seemed to enhance the melodious atmosphere of an already excited gathering of light.

Blues, reds, yellows, greens, whites and violets all came together, then flew apart like a spectacular fireworks display exploding across the ceiling of the cavern walls. Each light seemed to know what it was suppose to do, flying in directions that gave purpose and meaning.

Groups would form, split apart then come together again. Some would be motionless then zoom off to meet up with other particles of light, only to come back after a few moments and become motionless again. It all gave a new meaning to the dance of the bumble bee.

It was a hive of activity that no human had ever witnessed. A secret dance of light within a secret place.

The lights came from the mythical creatures called faeries or fae. Mystical and magical beings that help and work side by side with Mother Nature.

They are also the protectors of humans.

When the farmer fields his crops, they invisibly help by making sure the crop is in good condition. The cows are in good health, and that there is also a good and rich supply of herbs growing across the land.

Everyone was happy getting the cavern ready for the celebrations for the forth coming festival that was due in a few days. A celebration of the beginning of a new season. A very important time of the year for all faeries and humans, alike.

The faery in-charge of the organising and designing of this years celebration and every other past celebrations, was Faery Lammas Hoaky. His name means, 'Loaf mass' and 'Festival' so, by the nature of his name he was qualified to organise the celebration, and he did so with a happy heart and a humble spirit.

Elder Barren Strawberry flew over to talk to Lammas Hoaky, "Hello Lammas," Lammas stopped what he was doing and flew to meet Elder Strawberry.

"Hello my friend," Lammas said, "What brings you here? Are you trying to stop what has begun?"

"Nothing can stop this celebration, especially when you are the one who is organising it." Strawberry cheerfully said.

"I think this year's celebration is going to be quite earth shattering!"

- 21 FOREVER FRIENDS -

Years passed and as Solomon was growing up, his visits to the wood became less and less as school took over.

Dave set up his own business and was doing very well. As for Sarah, her painting courses became very popular with many people travelling from up and down England.

Solomon was sent to a private school and excelled. He grew up to be a fine young man, and in time joined his father in his business. As a past time, he would keep up with is own paintings, a gift he had picked up from his mother. He also had a talent for writing. It was only when he would come back to the house in Birchover village that he would write.

Solomon wrote stories that entertained children, and these stories centred around characters set in a wood. The stories focused on four main characters. They were called, Elder Perennial Swallowtail. Zeal White Oak. Balamore Skullcap and Solomon's favourite, Caitlin Lavender.

Often, Solomon would think about his friends, but it had been a long time since he had visited the wood. In time, his hobby of writing became a full time job since his stories were published and sold. Children from everywhere read them.

Sarah and Dave had moved out of the Birchover house to a bigger one, somewhere in Derbyshire. Solomon had been given the old house he had lived in from a child, because he felt he couldn't let it go.

He was now 33 years old and a successful children's writer. As time went on, his stories became just stories to him. The memories of years ago, became just stories and Solomon sometimes found it hard to think why the wood was special to him.

One day, as he was writing a new story a robin landed on the window sill of the living room, where he was writing. The window was open, and the robin started to sing. This got his attention immediately, and as he looked and saw the robin, he was amazed at the beauty.

The robin didn't stop singing when Solomon looked at it, but started to walk up and down the window sill. Solomon moved closer, and still the robin continued to sing and walk.

It was only when Solomon was a few inches away from the bird, that the robin flew away and nestled in a nearby tree, still singing and walking up and down a branch.

Solomon was mesmerised by this, and walked out and up to the robin. Again, the robin flew away but only flew a few feet, landing on another tree. Still singing and walking up and down the tree branch. Solomon felt he had to follow.

The robin would continually let Solomon come up to it until he was only a few inches away. It would then fly off, perch on another tree branch, sing and walk. Solomon followed until the robin took him away from his back garden and into the wood. When Solomon found himself standing in the wood and away from his house, he looked around and shrugged his shoulders. He walked deeper into the wood following the robin.

The robin now flew further into the woodland, leaving Solomon to follow until he was very far from his house. After a while, Solomon kept looking and saw no sign of the robin. As he was walking, he didn't see a tree stump jutting out of the ground and walked into it, tripping over and falling on his face. He quickly got up and brushed away the loose soil that was on his jumper. He sat down on an old tree that had fallen down many years ago.

"What am I doing here?" he said to himself.

Just then, he felt a little breeze on his face and from a distance, he could see something white flying towards him.

Solomon looked and stared at the oncoming object.

The object kept coming closer, then it stopped short of his face and dropped at his feet. He picked it up and turned it over. It was a picture, "OH MY!" he said out loud.

Solomon held it up in-front of his face. The picture was of a boy, surrounded by what looked like faeries. Solomon placed a finger on one of the faeries and said in a quiet voice, "Caitlin."

A tear fell from his left eye and flowed down his cheek. He then heard a voice.

"Don't cry Solomon. I'm here."

He looked up from the picture and saw hovering just a little away from his nose, was the most beautiful, graceful and gentle looking woman he had ever seen. She moved closer and gently kissed him on the nose.

With a face of shock, he said, "Caitlin!"

A beaming smile covered his face.

"It has been a long time Solomon," Caitlin said.

Solomon burst into tears. He was then surrounded by a larger gathering of faeries, who dried his tears and helped him up.

Solomon faced them all. Struggling to get his words out, he said to them all, "I...I'm sorry. I forgot you."

"No you didn't," Caitlin said, "You could never forget us."

"But, I haven't been here for such a long time," Solomon replied.

"But you have."

"How?"

Solomon was a little confused.

Caitlin lifted up the drawing that Solomon had in his hand, and then his face shone brightly and understood.

"My stories!"

All the faeries were cheering, and one came forward. It was Elder Perennial Swallowtail. He looked at Solomon.

"Again, thank you Solomon for keeping the magic alive."

Solomon then understood everything.

He was meant to write the stories, to keep the children knowing about the ones that look after everyone.

When we are lost in the wood, or when we have nightmares at night. They are the ones that keep us from harm when we are children.

That day in the wood woke Solomon up. Never did he forget the faeries, or the dragons or the oakmen. In-fact, Solomon made it his business to visit that wood everyday, just to say hello to it.

Solomon was special, and all mythical creatures and the creatures of the wood knew it.

Every time Solomon had a window open, he would be visited by an animal of the wood. If there was ever a storm, Solomon would leave his back door open to allow badgers, foxes and rabbits to seek shelter. He was especially happy if a faery or two flew in from the rain.

Occasionally, the faeries would contribute to new stories that Solomon would write, and they would show him more of their world. He always kept the most important parts of his times with the faeries a secret. Never writing it down, only keeping the experiences inside his head.

To the faeries Solomon was one of them, but only a little bit bigger! Even when the elders called meetings, they would always send out a few faeries to invite him to participate in the meetings. He always accepted. That's how close Solomon was to the faeries. They looked after him and he looked after them and the animals of the wood.

In time, Solomon married and had three children of his own. His wife and children also met Elder Perennial Swallowtail, Zeal White Oak, Balamore Skullcap, Sup Sup Rose and of course, Solomon's most precious friend, Caitlin Lavender.

To Solomon, and all that lived in the wood, the magic was still alive and would never die.

The End.

Author's Information

If you want to contact the author then you can by visiting the following web addresses.

Facebook
www.facebook.com/isrutter

Facebook Fan Pages – The Faeries of Birchover Wood
http://alturl.com/cthx8

Original:
https://www.facebook.com/pages/The-Faeries-of-Birchover-Wood/397556786944411

Personal website
www.iansrutter.co.uk/blog

My website has free written and video tutorials on how to create your own ebook.

I hope you have enjoyed this book, as it has been a great pleasure to write.